F

Supporting Learning in Schools

Hampshire
County Council

H005074741
Schools Library Service

Books by F. E. Higgins

The Phenomenals series

A Tangle of Traitors

A Game of Ghouls

The Tales from the Sinister City series

The Black Book of Secrets

The Bone Magician

The Eyeball Collector

The Lunatic's Curse

www.fehiggins.com

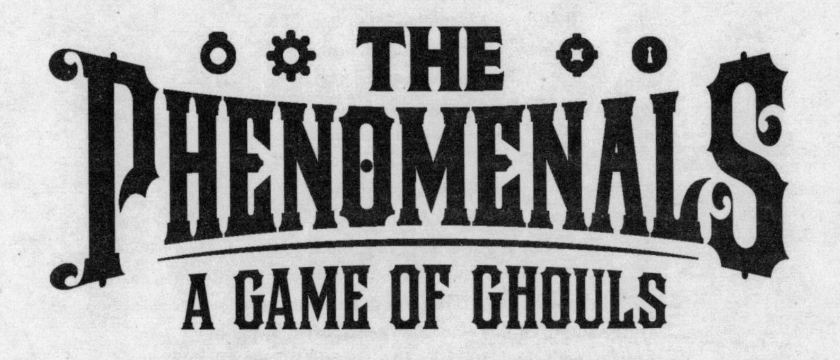

F. E. HIGGINS

MACMILLAN CHILDREN'S BOOKS

First published 2013 by Macmillan Children's Books
a division of Macmillan Publishers Limited
20 New Wharf Road, London N1 9RR
Basingstoke and Oxford
Associated companies throughout the world
www.panmacmillan.com

ISBN 978-0-330-50756-1

Copyright © F. E. Higgins 2013

The right of F. E. Higgins to be identified as
the author of this work has been asserted by her in
accordance with the Copyright, Designs and Patents Act 1988.

All rights reserved. No part of this publication may be
reproduced, stored in or introduced into a retrieval system, or
transmitted, in any form or by any means (electronic, mechanical,
photocopying, recording or otherwise), without the prior written
permission of the publisher. Any person who does any unauthorized
act in relation to this publication may be liable to criminal
prosecution and civil claims for damages.

1 3 5 7 9 8 6 4 2

A CIP catalogue record for this book is available from
the British Library.

Printed and bound by CPI Group (UK) Ltd, Croydon CR0 4YY

HAMPSHIRE SCHOOLS LIBRARY SERVICE	
H005074741	
Askews & Holts	03-Sep-2013
JF TEENAGE 11-14	£5.99

To Sarah and Aisling
Giorraíonn beirt bóthar

Contents

Author's Note

For those of you who are new to the world of Degringolade and the Supermundane I have included a glossary at the end of the book where you will find definitions of rare words and explanations for some of the more peculiar habits of Degringoladians and their unusual beliefs.

F. E. Higgins

Mangledore /*`man-gul-dore*/, rarely /*`man-gluh-dore*/

n. The cleanly severed, pickled hand of a convicted, executed criminal, in particular a murderer. The pickling process varies from region to region, but most often involves brown vinegar, sesame seeds and zimort. It is common practice for the fingers to be fixed round a candle (made from the rendered fat of a dead man), but occasionally the index finger is threaded with a wick. Once alight the candle ensures that all sleeping members of a household remain in a state of lethargic somnolence, thus enabling the holder to burgle without fear of discovery. The candle can be quenched only by milk

Chapter 1

An Unexpected Encounter

Folly laughed softly, if a little bitterly, to herself as she watched the blue Puca lights flitting bewitchingly ahead of her, always out of reach, trying to lure her away from the path across Palus Salus, the treacherous salt marsh of Degringolade. In truth, she was grateful for their company. The roof of the world had been swept across with a broad brush dipped in thick black paint from a palette of shades of darkness. Neither star nor planet nor celestial body of any kind was visible. She licked her lips. Usually she tasted salt in the air, but now there was something different, a sort of metallic tang.

'Odd,' she mused, and carried on, keen to get back to the Kryptos. Folly carried a manuslantern, which glowed softly at her side, but it struggled to illuminate the ground more than a few feet ahead of her. The Puca lights had that strange quality that their own brightness cast no light on their surroundings. That's why people end up in difficulty, thought Folly. They followed the blue flames not realizing that they were being led into peril. She was wise to their trickery.

'You'll not trip me up,' she called out gaily and, as if in cheeky reply, the flares danced even more wildly.

Then, without warning, they were extinguished.

Folly stopped dead in her tracks. Her breath, already clouding, seemed to freeze. She held up the manuslantern, but it was as if its light was swathed by gauze. She heard a soft sound, and felt the gentlest of breezes at the side of her face, followed immediately by a sharp crack as the lantern globe shattered, showering her cheek with jagged fragments of glass. She leaped back instinctively, releasing her hold on the lantern. It fell in a puddle of marsh water. The flame sputtered briefly and went out.

'Domna,' she hissed, admonishing herself for her unusual clumsiness. She turned her head slowly from left to right, her senses on high alert. Fear touched her heart, not because she was alone in the impenetrable darkness, *but because she wasn't.*

Slowly, Folly inserted her hand under the front of her long leather coat and pulled out her Blivet. It was cold to the touch, and if there had been even the smallest amount of light its triplet tines would have sparkled like the low Gevra morning sun on a frozen pond. She gripped the rare weapon tightly and steadied her breathing, forcing herself to remain calm. She knew her situation was perilous. Someone, *something*, was nearby, and its intent was indubitably malevolent.

She listened for any sound at all that might tell her in which direction her enemy lay. She was not expecting to hear breathing; the dead have no need of air. Neither did she anticipate footsteps; bodies that don't strike the ground create no noise. But there was something else, a thrumming, an almost tangible reverberation of the atmosphere around her. Experience told her this could mean only one thing. Somewhere in the nearby environs there was a Superent, a creature of the world of the Supermundane. There was no odour, and this was mildly worrying. Some believed that the smell of a Superent was inversely proportional to its malevolence: the less it stank the more dangerous it was. What Folly badly needed was light. It was not impossible to battle an invisible enemy, but it certainly wasn't easy.

The taste in her mouth was stronger now and she grimaced. With her free hand she felt in a pocket and her searching fingers closed over a stunner. It was a small weapon, no larger than a walnut, but its size belied its strength. It wasn't specifically designed to repel Superents, unlike the black beans and Natron she always carried (tonight she had the feeling that even a sackful of black beans and a dozen sprays of Natron would not deter this thing), but to shock. Still brandishing the Blivet, Folly threw the stunner at the ground in front of her. It exploded on contact with a loud bang and lit up the surrounding marsh with a bright white light. Folly could only hope it would last long enough to expose the Superent so at least she would know what she was dealing with.

It did, and the sight of her enemy caused Folly's stomach to lurch.

The creature was right in front of her. It must have been ten feet tall, muted green in colour, like pottery glaze, and shaped like a viscous liquid being poured from a height out of a glass. It had a face of sorts, complete with eyes and mouth, set within its large, wobbling torso. There were no discernible limbs and it moved as one mass of flesh. Folly, momentarily rooted to the spot, let out an involuntary gulp. She was no stranger to Superents, those baneful entities that were spawned from and inhabited the world of the Supermundane, but this was unlike any she had come across before. When, seconds later, the light faded, she was happy in some ways not to have to gaze upon its vile aspect any longer.

At last her sense of self-preservation took over, but it was almost too late. Just as the thing threatened to engulf her in its jellied folds of flabby corpulence, she covered her face with one hand and thrust the Blivet directly, with the confidence and deft execution that come only with practice, into the centre of the creature's globular trunk. With a terrible screech of pain or anguish the Superent toppled forward on to Folly. She crouched down helplessly. It was too late to run. She

feared she might not bear its weight, that she would suffocate beneath its mass. The thing covered her and it was like being engulfed in calf's foot jelly. But the cold was so intense that it was burning her. Despite an almost overwhelming urge to scream, Folly managed to keep her mouth firmly shut. Her lungs were heaving, but she knew that whatever she did, if she was to have any hope of survival, she must not inhale this toxic substance. The pain in her chest was intensifying. She didn't know how much longer she could stay like this. Just when she thought she might pass out, the Superent seemed to melt, as ice changes to water, and she found herself kneeling, an arm across her head, in a pool of repulsive, stringy mucus.

Gasping for breath, Folly sat back and thoroughly cleaned the revolting goo from her face, making sure not to lick her lips. Instantly all around her the Puca flared up and continued with their merry dance.

'Well, kew very much,' muttered Folly with sarcastic gratitude, staggering to her feet. It was disturbingly quiet. Not even the Lurids were howling. Had the wind changed? As if sensing that the danger was over, the clouds had moved on and the stars had chosen to reappear. She struck a Fulger's Firestrike and by its light found the broken manuslantern on the ground. She could replace the glass later, but for now she just lit the wick, careful to keep her distance from the naked flame. She could see the silhouette of a group of trees ahead

and knew that she was close to the Komaterion. She set off again, staying on the path, dripping goo and curling her lip at the thought of what she had just endured. One question plagued her the whole way.

What in Aether had just attacked her?

Chapter 2
A Good Vintage

While Folly was engaged in her near-fatal battle on the salt marsh with the unidentified Superent, Vincent Verdigris, the erstwhile 'Pilfering Picklock', was having a rather less life-threatening time in Degringolade city.

He was standing at the sturdy wooden door of the magnificent wine cellar of a noted local wine merchant, Webster Salmanazar. This wasn't the first time he had broken in to this cellar, but tonight he had been surprised to find that the locks had all been reinforced. He grinned, undeterred; if anything he was flattered, for this extra security was surely only put in place because of the *Degringolade Daily*'s constant warnings about Vincent's lock-picking skills. Since his arrival in the city there had been a spate of burglaries. Many were down to him, but equally many were copycat crimes carried out by less skilful thieves hoping the blame would be placed on Vincent. Vincent was both amused and annoyed by this, and very pleased when the copycats were exposed. He did not want his reputation tarnished by amateurs. The *Degringolade*

Daily had started a campaign in conjunction with a city locksmith, Will Van Clefhole & Son, to encourage the citizens to secure their homes until the 'Phenomenals', as Vincent and his three companions were now known, had been caught and thrown into the Degringolade penitentiary.

Earlier that evening Vincent had sat in what he liked to call his 'eyrie' (shared with a noisy flock of black corvids) behind the Kronometer overlooking the market square. From the heights of this lofty clock tower he had watched with a smile the scurrying Degringoladians as they emerged from Van Clefhole's shop with extra keys and padlocks. He had noted too the comings and goings of the locksmith's liveried cart and horse as it went about its business securing city properties.

Vincent laughed at the citizens' naivety. All this extra security had an almost negligible effect on his activities. Granted it might slow him down a little, but he was so proficient at every aspect of breaking and entering that he paid it little heed. Van Clefhole and his son were not fools. They could see a business opportunity when it presented itself and were taking full advantage of the citizens' fears. They weren't installing anything that Vincent hadn't come across before. In effect, they were merely doubling or tripling up on what was already there. Vincent was sorely tempted to break in to the locksmith's. It didn't seem right that they should

profit quite so much from his crimes.

So, perhaps he hummed to himself a split second longer as he picked at the wine-cellar lock with the treen tools he had inherited from his father, but that was about the long and the short of it.

Once inside he locked the door again as he always did; it warned him if someone was coming, gave him extra time to hide or escape, and occasionally deterred someone from investigating an unexplained noise because of the very fact that the door was secure. He tapped his smitelight against his leg and instantly it revealed his surroundings. He would be eternally grateful to Jonah for retrieving the small device from Kamptulicon. A precious gift from his father, the ingenious light continued to serve him well.

He went quickly to the racks where row upon row of fine wines in dusty bottles lay waiting for him. Red and white and rosé, sweet, dry, sparkling and fortified, they were all there. Folly's rabbit slumgullion benefited greatly from the addition of a full-bodied red, and Jonah's fish stews (using stolen fish, of course) were given an extra dimension from a splash of a light white. He himself had tried his hand at horsemeat pie with a glug of port and it had gone down very well indeed.

Absentmindedly Vincent rubbed his sleeve on the metal prosthetic attached to his right arm. It was a remarkable piece of craftsmanship, made from a strong yet light metal.

The removable fingers had jointed knuckles and responded readily to the flexing of his remaining digits within. The magnetic dial on the wrist had already proved its usefulness and he was quite certain that the hand had other tricks he had not yet discovered. He regretted the loss of his three fingers – of course he did – but he was getting used to it. Today he had attached all five false fingers and the hand resembled a metal glove. Oddly enough, the more he wore it, the less he was inclined to remove it. He had not been wearing it a full lunar cycle yet, but it was becoming an integral part of him. At night when he couldn't sleep he liked to imagine who had owned the artificial hand before him – a great inventor, perhaps, or maybe it was part of an Autandron, one of those moving metal men of which he had heard rumours. He made a mental note to ask Wenceslas Wincheap next time he was at the Caveat Emptorium.

Right now though, the still-healing wound was throbbing. He had done as Folly told him, soaking the raw flesh in salted water, smearing on a thick layer of soothing unguent and drinking the Antikamnial regularly. It was strong stuff, and the throbbing was a sign that its painkilling properties were wearing off.

Hungry and feeling more acutely the need for pain relief, Vincent turned to his task. He wanted to get back to the Kryptos before the Kronometer struck Mid-Nox. Quickly he

chose two bottles of wine, a red and a white – both, by the look of the fussy labels, of a very high quality – standing on a small tasting table at the end of the rack. He dropped them into the deepest pockets of his cloak and was about to leave when the sound of voices and a key in the door stopped him in his tracks. Whoever was on the other side was fumbling, giving Vincent valuable seconds to slip out of sight between the wine rack and the wall. He flattened himself against the cold stone, destroying cobwebs and sending spiders running. Vincent was unworried by the visitor, doubtless the merchant coming down for a bottle.

The door opened. 'The Lurids are quiet tonight,' said the first man to enter.

'Hmm,' replied a second voice, also male. 'Not a good sign.'

'This way, this way,' said the first man, rather excitedly, closing the door. 'I left them out for you. The tasters report it to be the best yet from that year.'

'Excellent, excellent,' came the reply. 'The thought of just a sip of it has me all a-tremble!'

Except he didn't say 'tremble', he said 'tremmel', which caused Vincent to groan inwardly. He would know that speech impediment anywhere: Governor Leucer d'Avidus.

Vincent frowned. This was an unexpected turn. He, Folly, Jonah and Citrine knew that Leucer d'Avidus was

inextricably linked with Leopold Kamptulicon and the Lurid and the fiasco down at the Tar Pit, and any man who claimed acquaintance with both Kamptulicon and Edgar Capodel could not be trusted at all.

Through the small gaps in the rack Vincent watched the merchant approach the tasting table. This simple action elicited a second silent groan as his fear was realized.

'There were two,' the merchant was saying. 'A white and a red. I left them here.'

Leucer was beginning to get impatient, as evidenced by his tapping foot and its echo around the damp cellar. 'Perhaps they have been stolen.'

The merchant started. 'You mean by that Vincent fellow? But how? I have installed new locks all over the place.'

'He and his little band of cronies are not called the Phenomenals for nothing,' replied Leucer thoughtfully. 'I hardly need to remind you, the particular skill of a Phenomenal is to come and go as it pleases without being seen. The Urban Guardsmen have not caught them yet and there have been no sightings. There is speculation that they have left the city, but we know that the boy, Vincent, is still here. He is like a sharp stone in my shoe.'

Vincent smiled. He was quite happy to be a stone in Leucer's expensive shoes. He watched as Leucer turned up his own manuslantern and stared hard at the floor.

‘Who has access to this cellar?’

‘Nanyone except me. It stores my most expensive wines.’

‘Well, unless you have feet of different sizes, I suggest that someone other than you has been down here.’ Leucer pointed to the floor and both men stared hard at the sets of small and big footprints in the dust. Vincent dug his nails, metal fingers and all, into his palms in irritation at his own carelessness. The light in the cellar was poor, deliberately so to protect the wine, and he had not bothered to conceal his tracks.

‘I see nany prints leaving,’ observed Leucer slyly.

‘You mean the thief *might still be here*?’ whispered the merchant. ‘Shouldn’t we call the guardsmen? There’s a reward!’

Vincent made a face. Last he heard, the reward was one thousand sequenturies. A fair amount, a compliment to his lock-picking in fact, but he had no intention of lining anyone’s pockets. He watched with mounting unease as Leucer drew a long-barrelled pistol. The governor advanced along the racks, gesturing to the merchant to stand guard at the door.

Silently, smoothly and reluctantly, Vincent drew his own weapon, a treen dagger carved from Gaboon ebony. His heart was heavy. ‘Only amateurs steal with violence,’ his father used to say. ‘A real thief comes and goes like a shadow. There is no need for anyone to be hurt.’

Vincent sized up his opponents. He could see from the

merchant's quivering lip and shaking hands that he had no stomach for a fight. The governor, however, was another matter.

'Come out, boy,' called Leucer. 'I know you're in there.'

Vincent steadied his breathing and tightened his grip around his knife. 'Sorry, Father,' he said silently, 'but this is the way it has to be.' The cellar was windowless, there was only one way out and Leucer stood between him and it.

Light glinted off the shining barrel of Leucer's pistol as he advanced, but Vincent still had the element of surprise. He took a deep breath, issued a mighty roar and rushed head down at the oncoming enemy.

But before either could strike a blow or fire a shot, there was the most tremendous rumble and the cellar shook violently from side to side. The ground shuddered like the stiffened legs of a donkey being pulled where it didn't want to go. Vincent was amazed to see a ripple cross the floor, like a wave in a pool. Everything seemed to be moving.

Over the deep roaring there came the higher-pitched noise of glass breaking. Wine bottles, shaken from the racks, were crashing one after another to the hard stone floor, shattering on impact, showering Vincent and Leucer and the merchant with their aromatic contents. Corks were popping at random and shooting around the cellar. Vincent thought this was what it must be like to be under fire from a hundred pistols.

It was impossible to stay upright and all three fell to the ground. Vincent found himself lying only feet away from Leucer, staring straight into the man's eyes. Leucer was holding on to the wine rack with one hand and brandishing the pistol in the other.

'Got you now, you scullion!' roared the governor. He took aim as well as he could under the unsteady circumstances and Vincent could see his finger starting to squeeze the trigger. Desperately he tried to get to his feet. Then, unbelievably, a jagged-edged chasm opened up in the floor between them. The force of the fracture sent Leucer rolling helplessly in one direction and Vincent in the other.

As quickly as it had started, the rumbling stopped and the ground settled.

Clouds of dust swirled around the room. Panting and coughing, Vincent got to his feet. Leucer was on one knee across the chasm, searching the sticky, glass-smithereened floor around him for his weapon. He snarled at Vincent as his hand closed over the pistol.

'So long, guv,' said Vincent with a grin and a wink. Then, as Leucer aimed the pistol at his head, he bounded over the prostrate merchant and made good his escape through the doorway, the ringing report of pistol fire in his wake.

CHAPTER 3

THE WILD CARD

Citrine reached up to scratch her head and uttered a small sound of irritation. Whatever was in the hair dye was causing her head to itch. She pulled her hood forward again, just brushing her silver browpin with its onyx stone. It gave her a little comfort. Few Degringoladians went without some sort of protective talisman: bejewelled browpins or large-stoned rings were favoured by the rich, men and women alike; earrings or less ostentatious pendants were worn by others.

She looked up again at the dark building a hundred yards or so down the street: the Capodel Townhouse, the finest house in the city. She used to stand on the balcony and count the beams of the lighthouse until her father returned from the manufactory. Her heart hardened at the memory. That was before Cousin Edgar had so cruelly betrayed her and forced her out of her home. Now two burly guards stood stolidly on the other side of imposing wrought-iron gates.

'Looks like nanyone's home,' said Jonah beside her.

'Edgar's probably at the Bonchance Club.'

‘You know Vincent can get in, take anything you want. By the multitudes of mackerel in the seven seas, his thieving skills have not let us down yet.’

‘Hmm,’ murmured Citrine, thinking of the collection of browpins, among other things, that she had left behind in her old bedroom. She hadn’t quite got the measure of Vincent Verdigris yet. Yes, he provided well for them all; food and drink and a whole raft of practical items that were lacking in Folly’s now rather crowded tomb-home, and he loved to tell tales, tall tales, but she couldn’t help feeling that the outward bravado was a mask, that there was more below the surface.

Folly, however, was a different kettle of fish. She was a listener, not a talker. She nodded at Vincent’s stories, but withheld her own. Citrine suspected she had plenty to rival his. Vincent wouldn’t like that. He was the sort of fellow who couldn’t resist a challenge, no matter how uncertain the outcome.

‘We should get on to Suma’s,’ urged Jonah, interrupting her thoughts. He was growing anxious. The Degringolade Urban Guardsmen (DUG for short but more often referred to as Urgs) were extra vigilant these days, all on the lookout for the Phenomenals, and of the quartet he was undoubtedly the most recognizable.

‘I just wish I knew what Edgar is up to,’ said Citrine quietly.

Jonah looked at her sideways. *And whether or not your father really is dead.*

It was snowing again as they hurried away. Citrine was slightly ahead of Jonah and reached the street where they had parked the Trikuklos first. It was not an easy conveyance to conceal, but Jonah had reached up and quenched the nearby lights to that end. She was only feet away when a figure stepped out from behind it. She slowed, recognizing the silhouette of the cap of a member of the DUG.

'Is this your vehicle?'

Jonah, lagging behind, heard the voice and backed off. 'Codtails, an Urg!' he muttered, making the word an expression of disgust.

Citrine swallowed hard and wiped melting snow from her face, suddenly aware of a burning sensation spreading across her cheeks.

'Someone has vandalized the street lights down here. Dangerous times. You've heard of those Phenomenals?'

Citrine nodded earnestly. 'I don't want to come across one of their lot!'

The guardsman held up his standard-issue manuslantern to look at her more closely. 'Hang about, lass, what's that on your face?'

Citrine saw then that her hand was streaked with black.

Her cheeks were now stinging painfully. *Domna! The dye!*

The Urg's expression changed slowly, as if he was wrestling with a tricky mathematical problem. 'Your hair, it's changing colour!' he said dully.

Citrine looked down at her hair, to her horror now streaked with red.

The Urg took a step towards her and his face lit up. He had worked it out. 'Domne! You're the red-haired Phenomenal! *You're Citrine Capodel.*'

He put his whistle to his mouth, but before he could blow it Jonah loomed large and rushed him, knocking him to the ground. Then he dragged Citrine into the Trikuklos and was already pedalating away even as she struggled to pull the door to.

'They already believe you're a murderer,' said Jonah grimly. 'Adding assault of an Urg to your record won't make much difference.' Then, seeing the distressed look on her face, he added, 'He'll be fine. I saw him get up in the mirror.'

The pair fell silent and did not speak again until they reached Mercator Square. Jonah manoeuvred the vehicle between the stalls, finally stopping at the side of a black kite wagon set back from the main thoroughfare. A large corvid on the roof eyed them intelligently. 'Let's not be too long,' warned Jonah, 'or Folly'll be complaining.'

Citrine smiled briefly. She knew what Jonah meant. The

atmosphere in the Kryptos was becoming a little strained. Folly got tetchy when her guests went out and didn't come back at the appointed time.

She raised her fist to knock, but before her knuckles could make contact with the wood the door was swiftly opened and Citrine's heart soared at the sight of Suma Dartson, the finest card-spreader in Degringolade.

'My, oh my, but what a time it's been,' declared Suma, pulling them both in and closing the louvred door behind them (no easy task with a fellow the size of Jonah in the way). She picked curiously at a strand of Citrine's straggly black and russet hair.

'The dye ran,' explained the bedraggled girl.

Suma handed her a damp cloth to clean up, and while Citrine engaged in her ablutions the old lady turned to Jonah. 'Dear Jonah, or should I call you "Brute"!' she said. 'Your names and pictures are all over this city.'

Behind her, Citrine's face fell. 'We'll leave, if you think we might get you into trouble.'

Suma looked shocked. 'Oh, my dear, I would never turn you away! You'll want your cards spread, I expect. I'm ready.' She nodded to a felt-topped card table. 'But first, tell me, what exactly happened to you all down at the Tar Pit? The *Degringolade Daily* is not a paper where truth and reality are harmonious bedfellows.'

Citrine sensed, as usual, that the wrinkled old lady knew more than she let on, but indulged her. Quickly she related everything that had happened since her last visit: how Edgar had betrayed her and brought about her imprisonment; how Jonah had saved her from the noose (and then saved Vincent from Kamptulicon and Folly from the Lurid at the Ritual of Appeasement); and about the discovery of her father's empty casket in the Capodel family tomb.

'And now,' she ended, on a note of quiet despair, 'we're fugitives. I still don't know if my father is dead or alive; I have been convicted of murdering poor dear Florian, father's solicitor; and Edgar has inherited everything. Folly says Leopold Kamptulicon is a Cunningman – she knows about these things – and that he and Edgar and Governor d'Avidus are plotting something terrible.'

Suma put her arm round Citrine's shaking shoulders and spoke gently. ''Tis no wonder you're out of sorts. You have been treated most unfairly.'

Jonah slid down in a chair near the stove and rubbed his rough hands together to warm them. The sound was like a carpenter planing a plank of treen. A whistling started up and Suma took the kettle off the stove. She made three mugs of tea and handed them around.

Jonah asked, 'What do you know of Leucer d'Avidus? Does he ever come to you?'

'If he did, I couldn't tell you,' replied Suma. 'My clients expect privacy, you understand. I can only say of him what I read in the paper.'

Jonah snorted. 'Hah, the *Degringolade Daily* never has a bad word to say about him. He's filthy rich, that much is known to all, from the spoils of the Tar Pit. Though Poseidon knows how he came to own it – it's on Degringolade land.'

Citrine noticed that his voice sounded different, somehow clearer, and realized that for once he didn't have his coat collar pulled up around his scarred face.

Suma's brow creased.'The water, or perhaps I should say "tar", is rather muddied when it comes to Leucer d'Avidus and his business interests.'

Citrine was no longer listening: her attention had been caught by something else: Suma's leech barometer. Inside the tall bell jar on the shelf, twelve black bloodsuckers were writhing themselves into a frenzied knot, slime oozing out from between their sinuated bodies.

'Nothing is behaving as it should,' said Suma. 'The Lurids are almost silent, the corvids on the Kronometer are very unsettled and the leeches have been knotting like that all day.'

Citrine shuddered and averted her eyes from the glistening entanglement. 'It's giving me nerves just looking at them,' she muttered. 'Can we spread the cards now?'

Jonah had succumbed to the soporific warmth of the

wagon and drifted off into oceanic reveries. Suma lit a carved candle in the middle of the card table and Citrine pulled up a stool. She placed a green bag in front of her, but Suma stopped her.

'I have some new cards I would like to try. Wenceslas found them in the Caveat Emptorium. They'd been there so long he couldn't remember where they came from. But we'll use your maerl dice.'

Citrine took four small stone-like objects from her bag, each with a different number of sides, and rolled three across the table. She totalled the vertical lines on show, five in all, then she threw the remaining thirteen-sided piece of maerl. It tumbled to a standstill with the symbol of a spider uppermost. 'Arachnoid spread,' she said, and arranged ten of the faded purple-backed cards in a pattern on the table.

Citrine was hopeful that for once the cards would hold some good news. She picked five from the spread, turned them over one at a time and laid them in a straight line. On the turn of the fifth she uttered a little sound of surprise. 'It's some sort of beast! That card's not in my deck.'

Suma sucked noisily through the gaps in her teeth. It was not unusual to come across new cards. All packs included a set of standard characters, but the rest differed from region to region.

'It's certainly an ugly thing,' she began, but was immediately

interrupted by a loud squawk and a scrabbling noise from the roof. Suddenly the wagon wobbled dangerously and threatened to go right over.

Citrine reeled and grabbed at the table. Suma gripped the armrests of her chair in alarm. Jonah awoke, wide-eyed and staring, and jumped to his feet crying, 'Batten down the hatches! Rope her, lads, rope her!' before realizing that he was not in a storm at sea but in Suma's wagon.

A deep rolling roar filled their ears and the wagon shook violently for a full thirty seconds. Citrine recovered her balance just in time to prevent the leech barometer from smashing to the floor.

And then it was all over.

Citrine straightened cautiously. 'Domna, was that an earthquake?'

Jonah, a little embarrassed by his performance, scooped up a set of scattered Cachelot teeth and replaced them on the shelf.

'This *is* Degringolade,' said Suma, as if that was all the explanation needed.

Badly unsettled by the quake, the cards forgotten for now, Jonah and Citrine were anxious to leave.

'Come back whenever you can,' said Suma, bustling them down the steps. 'And don't forget Wenceslas Wincheap at the Caveat Emptorium. He will gladly help you with anything

you need. A fellow in his trade knows more 'n most folk about the doings in this city. Just mention my name.'

People were coming out of their houses and shops. A small crowd had gathered under the Kronometer, pointing and gabbling excitedly. The luminous hands were just approaching Mid-Nox, but the black pendulum that usually hissed softly from left to right was still. For now, time in Degringolade was no longer measured by the Kronometer; it had stopped.

'Go,' urged Suma, 'before you're seen.'

The old woman stood on the steps and watched the pair pedalate away. She looked again at the beast card in her hand.

'Katatherion,' she said thoughtfully, 'depicted in slumber, a great danger waiting to be woken.'

Chapter 4

Only in Degringolade . . .

Leopold Kamptulicon stood on the charred and desolate edge of the Tar Pit of Degringolade and looked out across the oily black surface of the lake. He allowed himself a moment or two of self-indulgence as he recalled again the incredible sense of power that had engulfed him – yes, engulfed; there was no other word to describe the feeling – when, at his very command, he had watched the Lurid of Axel Harpelaine assume the body of his living sister, Folly. It was a sight Leopold would never forget. It might have been a short-lived triumph, Jonah – the 'Brute' – had made sure of that, but he still took great pleasure in knowing what it was like to have a Lurid completely under his control.

He tutted and shook his head. Luck was a fickle lady and she had chosen that night of all nights to play with him. It was undoubtedly serendipity that the random Lurid he had summoned from the horde out on the tar was Folly Harpelaine's brother. This blood tie ensured that Folly could easily be used as a vessel for Axel's restless spirit. In fact, she

was even better than his original choice, Vincent Verdigris. But then all this good fortune was countered by the fact that the Mangledore, the herbally steeped and ritually waxed severed hand of an executed criminal, belonged to that very same brother. When the Brute had tossed it into the lake, Folly had been instantly released from Kamptulicon's power.

Who in Aether could ever have imagined such a twisted set of circumstances?

'Only in Degringolade,' muttered Leopold as he watched again in his mind's eye the Mangledore sailing in a perfect arc through the air to land in the sticky sucking muck. And as he re-imagined it sinking below the surface, so too his heart plummeted in his chest.

Leopold blamed everything on Vincent, the thieving wretch with the metal arm. At the time he had been delighted to catch the young intruder in his underground Ergastirion, the workshop where he kept his Supermundane paraphernalia, but the boy was proving to be more trouble than he was worth. True, it wasn't Vincent who had actually tossed the Mangledore into the tar and thus ruined all his plans, but he had masterminded it all; Leopold was convinced of it.

'I should have killed him when I had him strapped up in my chair,' he muttered. 'Freezing his fingers off was far, far less than he deserved.' On top of all that, Vincent had stolen his book, his precious Omnia Intum.

‘And the one-handed cullion still has it,’ hissed the thwarted Cunningman, unable to hold in his venom any longer at the thought of the powerful book, a book even he did not fully understand, in the hands of a lowly Vulgar. ‘I will get my book back,’ he vowed to the night, ‘if I have to throttle every domnable one of those Phenomenals.’

Kamptulicon could feel the residual heat of the fires through the thick soles of his boots, so he started to walk along the shore. He went slowly, raking absent-mindedly through the detritus with the metal-tipped point of his staff.

It was a relatively new acquisition, supporting both his body and his ego. He thought it gave him a degree of gravitas. Kamptulicon was concerned that he had lost some of the respect he had previously commanded, and undoubtedly deserved. Hadn’t he given Leucer what he had asked for, namely an embodied Lurid? And in doing so he had demonstrated that Leucer’s dream, a legion of such Lurids under his sole command, utterly biddable and needing no earthly sustenance, was close to becoming reality. That still hadn’t stopped him grumbling (‘grummling,’ sniggered Leopold) about the subsequent farrago at the Tar Pit.

As for Edgar Capodel, that louche fop, all he was interested in was gambling and drinking and being seen to be powerful. Well, there was a difference between having power and merely having its appearance. One day Edgar Capodel would realize

that. For now, he was oblivious to the fact that he was a mere puppet whose strings were being pulled by Leucer d'Avidus to gain access to the facilities and chemicals at the Capodel Manufactory.

Leopold Kamptulicon was feeling many things, but mainly frustration. 'I am a Cunningman!' he declared to the night. 'A master of the Supermundane, a manipulator of the hidden realms. Leucer does not pull my strings. But without an Ergastirion I am hindered, restrained in my powers.'

Indeed, that was the very reason he was in this desolate place, seeking out somewhere to set up a new workshop of evilry. He had fled his Ergastirion under the oil shop when Vincent had stumbled across it. For now, Edgar had allowed him to store his paraphernalia in a small unused storeroom at the Capodel Manufactory, but it was far from ideal. But this place would not do either, he decided.

The thwarted Cunningman returned to his black mare and rode off. At the broken archway of the Degringolade gate, an indication that he was almost back on the Great West Road, a thought came into his head. 'What about Degringolade Manor? Could that not serve as an Ergastirion?'

Excited at the prospect, Kamptulicon pulled on the reins, wheeled his horse round and started up the overgrown driveway to the derelict building, only to give up shortly after. The overgrowth and undergrowth were impenetrable. It must have been fifty years since Lord and Lady Degringolade had passed on. He hadn't been in the city when they were alive (but he like everyone else had heard the rumours of their eccentricities) and it looked as if no one had gone up to the house for decades.

Suddenly something small and fast dashed out from the long-thorned briars and ran right between the horse's legs. Startled, she snorted and danced about nervously, nearly unseating Kamptulicon. He managed to calm her, but as she settled he became aware of a strange noise, gathering rapidly in volume, apparently coming from the trees and bushes. It was a growing cacophony of scrabbling and scratching and squealing and hissing. Kamptulicon lifted his lantern and watched in amazement asa horde of four-legged animals of all shapes and sizes burst forth from the undergrowth and raced away like a moving carpet. At the same time above and all about his head he could hear and feel the flapping of scores of pairs of wings. He put his arms up to protect himself and could just see the silhouettes of perhaps a thousand birds in panicked flight. His horse became more and more agitated. Foam flecked her nostrils and the whites of her eyes were visible. He struggled to control her. His lantern swung at such an acute angle that it quenched itself, leaving the Cunningman effectively blind and fighting to stay in the saddle.

The ground began to shake. The mare reared and Kamptulicon was thrown violently to the ground. He heard the beast galloping away and he lay where he fell, winded. The earth's tremors went right through the soft marrow of his bones. Unable to stand, he clutched at his protective ring and shouted out harshly, over and over again, a virtually unintelligible sequence of words in Quodlatin.

CHAPTER 5
KATATHERION

In the middle of the black lake the Lurids huddled in uneasy anticipation. Above them the moon was now in its perigee phase, nearing the earth, and although men might gaze upon it in wonder and awe the Lurids feared the silvery disc, and its ever-closer presence caused them pain.

But the moon's increasing proximity was just one reason the Lurids were unsettled. The earthquake had greatly added to their agitation. And it was not only those who dwelt above the shifting ground who had been disturbed, but also those below. Somewhere deep in the subterranean realms of the salt marsh, in a damp and pitch-black cavern, a creature of horrific appearance was shaken and stirred by the earth's seismic shift.

It was a devilish beast, no doubt about that. It could be likened to a dog, if a dog had scaly skin.. It had jaws like a dog and it opened these jaws in a huge yawn, drawing its lips back from its yellow fangs and exposing its darkly red shining throat. When its mouth closed and the teeth came together,

four fangs remained visible, sliding down beside each other so tightly not even a flea's leg would have fitted in between.

The creature stretched like a cat waking after a long slumber, its claws scoring the ground deeply and its broad rump pushing upward. It stood up to its full height on four thick-thighed bristly legs. It was ill-tempered; it was hungry for sustenance; it wanted to be free.

Slowly, stiffly, it left the cavern and began its journey towards the surface.

Chapter 6
The Prophecy

Folly, still pondering her close encounter with the gelatinous Superent, was negotiating her way between the graves and monuments in the Komaterion when the earthquake struck. The squat, grey Kryptos was already in sight when she became aware that something was up, alerted by the scores of rabbits fleeing their burrows and bounding away, paying her no heed at all.

At the onset of the tremor Folly crouched low and steadied herself against a tree. This was not something she had experienced before and it took a great deal of self-control to quell the fear that surged in her veins. She was glad to be in the relative safety of the Komaterion rather than on the narrow marsh path where she could so easily have been tossed into the surrounding sucking mud pools. Though it might not have been such a bad thing if she had; to be covered in salty marsh mud was marginally better than the slimy Supermundane residue that coated her at present.

After a long thirty seconds, when terra firma really was

terra firma again, with her heart pummelling her ribs, Folly ran to the shelter of the Kryptos porch. From the outside the tomb looked unscathed by the geological assault, but the door was stiff. She suspected that it had shifted slightly on its hinges. Once inside she leaned against it to close it and finally allowed herself to relax, glad to breathe in the smell of what she considered home – the lingering aroma of slumgullion – and to hear the hum of the tar-powered Cold Cabinet (which Jonah had lugged from the Capodel Townhouse).

Folly glanced at the clock on the mantel – a delightful Ansonia swinger clock with a dainty cherub-like figure (purloined by Vincent, of course) – and realized that she hadn't heard the Kronometer ring in the hour. Perhaps the grumbling earth had drowned out its chimes. The others had promised to be back by Mid-Nox. She was annoyed that they were late, but part of her was glad to have the place to herself. Vincent wasn't the only one who valued his solitude.

Keen to clean herself up, Folly struck a firestrike and lit the wall lamps. With a certain degree of trepidation she looked around the chamber. One of the flagstones had split, over by the casket plinth they used as a table. Somewhat macabrely, Lady Degringolade's own casket had been shaken from its niche in the wall and now lay on its side on the floor. The lid had broken into four pieces and her disarticulated skeleton spewed forth in a confusion of bones.

Folly knelt to replace the bones in the casket and saw out of the corner of her eye that a piece of stone had been dislodged from the wall behind her pillow. She tutted. That was where she kept Kamptulicon's stolen Omnia Intum, in the cavity behind the stone. The small book was still there; she took it and put it in her pocket. Now that her hiding place was no longer secure, she would have to find somewhere better. The other three didn't know where she kept it, and that was how it should be. A Cunningman's handbook was a volume that deserved respect. Within its pages were centuries-old secrets, incantations and rituals of the Supermundane. She was certain that Kamptulicon would come looking for it before too long, and the fewer people who knew its hiding place the better. Unfortunately, the Kryptos was not designed to conceal secrets.

Still sticky with the Superent's goo, Folly put a large pot over the fire to heat some water. The door scraped open and Vincent, Citrine and Jonah came hurrying in.

'Sorry we're late . . .' began Citrine, and then she put her hand to her mouth in shock. 'What in Aether happened to you?'

Folly did indeed cut a rather bedraggled figure. 'I was attacked,' she said matter-of-factly, 'but the other one came off worse, believe me. I just need a wash.'

'Domne, so you felt it here too,' said Jonah, stepping into

the chamber, carefully avoiding the crack in the floor.

'You clean yourself up,' said Citrine, taking the slumgullion pot from the Cold Cabinet. 'I'll sort some food. Did you know the Kronometer's stopped?'

Folly looked at her sharply. 'Stopped?'

'Yes, the quake . . .' started Citrine, but Folly talked over her:

> '*Should ere this pendulum of blackened brass,*
> *No longer swing its graceful pass,*
> *Beware the risen Degringolade*
> *For blood will smear their sharpened blade!*'

'Oh goodness, the prophecy! I had forgotten all about that,' said Citrine.

'Prophecy?' Vincent looked astonished at Folly's spontaneous performance.

'It's associated with the Kronometer,' said Folly.

'Yes,' said Citrine. 'Everyone knows it here, but I haven't heard mention of it for years.'

Vincent laughed. 'A Degringolade will rise from the dead?' He pointed to Lady Degringolade's fallen casket and the bones within. 'I don't think there's much chance of that.'

Folly went to the trunk in the corner and pulled out some clean clothes. Jonah righted the coffin, replaced the lid as well as he could, like a badly fitting jigsaw, and shoved it up against the wall. He contemplated lifting it back into the niche. He knew he could, but he thought perhaps the cavity would make a good sleeping place for him. He couldn't get used to the floor and, though nothing would match the gentle swing of a hammock on a ship, the niche would surely be preferable.

Vincent was still in a state of exhilaration after his latest narrow escape. Luck was definitely on his side tonight. Not only had he escaped Leucer's bullet – admittedly the earthquake had played a part in that – but with remarkable serendipity he had entered Mercator Square just as Citrine and Jonah were taking off in the Trikuklos. What a shock he had given them when he had jumped out from behind a stall and asked for a ride. He was starting to think that being in a city as riven with superstition as Degringolade might not be such a bad thing. Certainly he had done well thieving. There was something about the atmosphere of Degringolade too, not just the wailing Lurids and the oily stink from the Tar Pit, that made him feel he could take chances he wouldn't normally. Jonah had called him foolish; he preferred to think of himself as daring and courageous.

He noticed, with a small sound of dismay, that the wall mirror was shattered. 'What happened here? Did you look in the mirror, Folly?' He enjoyed teasing the serious girl.

Folly, combing goo from her hair, was in no mood for levity. She gave him a withering look. 'Very funny. We're not all so concerned with our looks.'

Citrine shot an anxious look at Jonah, but he was busy investigating the damage and hadn't heard. She tried to catch Vincent's eye, but he was too wrapped up in laughing at his own joke.

It was no secret that he liked to look at himself, and Folly had scolded him more than once about his habit of leaving the mirror exposed. 'You know it's bad luck to leave mirrors uncovered at night,' she had said. 'You're just inviting Superents to come through.'

Vincent scoffed. Although he had become more accepting of the Degringoladians' superstitious way of life, and now agreed that Superents really did exist, he found this particular taboo tedious. Citrine, sensing Folly's irritation, tried to defuse the growing tension. 'So what exactly attacked you? A Lurid?

Folly shook her head. 'No, not a Lurid, something else. My father came home once covered with this muck. It's called "ghouze" and it's poisonous to eat. He told me the creature's name, but I can't remember it. I'm sure I saw a picture of it in the book.'

Folly ran her fingers through her damp blonde hair one last time, then took out Kamptulicon's book and flicked towards the end. Here there were many pages devoted wholly to creatures of the Supermundane, a gruesome litany of Superents.

'My word, but it's like Homer's catalogue of ships,' commented Citrine, and spent a few sombre seconds reminiscing about her schoolroom days. Folly pointed to an ink drawing of what could only be described as a shapeless blob. 'It was this one.'

'It doesn't look like it was ever a person. I always thought Superents were the shades of dead people.'

'Lurids are,' said Folly, 'but there are plenty of other Superents that were never human. This is a Pluribus. Listen.' She proceeded to read from the book:

'"Green in colour, a Pluribus (plural Pluriba) is composed of ghouze, a semi-liquefied Supermundane substance, created from invisible atmospheric particles called minuscules (thought to be the fifth state after solids, liquids, gases and plasma), which are attracted to each other whenever there is a disturbance of significance in the Supermundane world. Pluriba exist overground and are generally thought to be a harbinger of disaster or a malevolent event."'

Vincent snorted, annoyed that he hadn't yet had a chance to tell his story. 'Are you sure about that? I mean, this is Quodlatin after all. It could mean anything.'

Folly ignored the jibe, which referred to the time she

had mistranslated the deceptive language. 'It's not *all* in Quodlatin. Some of it is quite straightforward. It's the secret stuff, the rituals and mysteries, that can be confusing.'

'I wonder if it's all connected to Kamptulicon summoning the Lurid,' mused Citrine aloud, stirring the slumgullion. Folly continued to look through the book and Jonah was still on his hands and knees by the plinth. Vincent took out the bottles of wine from his pockets and set them down rather loudly on the table. 'Rather more appetizing than your ghoul goo,' he said.

Citrine was impressed. 'They look very good.' She noted the labels. 'I've seen ones like them in my father's cellar.'

'Only the best for Leucer d'Avidus.'

Folly closed the book. 'Leucer? Don't tell me you've been in the Governor's Residence.'

'No, at the wine merchant's, Salmanazar's. I've just had the narrowest escape ever.'

Jonah raised a sceptical eyebrow. 'Another one?'

'Leucer and the merchant came in. I had to fight them off.'

'You mean they saw you?' Folly sounded increasingly incredulous.

'I escaped just as the quake struck.' This wasn't exactly how it had happened, but Vincent was not going to allow Folly to spoil his moment of glory.

'He's not the only one to have had a narrow escape,' said Citrine. Unlike Vincent, her face reddened as she told Folly about the near miss with the Urban Guardsman.

Now Folly looked aghast. 'Are you sure you weren't followed? If the Urgs find us here, we're in big trouble. And you, Vincent, you're just reckless. You keep telling us how skilled you are, but next time you might not be so lucky. Nine lives 'n' all that.'

'Oh, crunk,' said Vincent rather rudely. 'I know what I'm doing. And you all benefit from the fruits of my little escapades: lanterns, food, drink. Who put you in charge anyway?'

'We *are* grateful for the things you bring back,' Citrine said quickly, and diplomatically, seeing the look on Folly's face, 'but we're a team now – that's all Folly's trying to say.'

'Some team! You're ganging up on me.'

'Well, what do you expect when you say you like to work alone,' said Folly, barely able to keep her temper.

'I don't have to stay here. I can leave any time.'

'Well, why don't you?'

'Fish-guts!' interrupted Jonah opportunely. 'I think these are hinges.'

He had taken up one half of the broken flagstone and was kneeling over the gap. The others crowded around him. He lifted the second piece and they all saw quite plainly what lay

beneath: a smooth, hinged stone slab, covered in years of dust and dirt. Folly rubbed the flat of her hand over the exposed surface and uncovered what looked like a recessed iron ring. She tried to prise it out, but it was stuck. Vincent flicked a switch on the wrist of his artificial hand and held it flat over the ring, which began to rise, drawn towards his hand by the powerful magnetic force. He smiled triumphantly, gripped the ring and pulled. But to no avail. He knew his limits and stepped back to allow the sailor to take over. Almost effortlessly Jonah pulled up the slab, raising a cloud of dust. All four leaned over the opening and peered into the darkness below.

'A secret passageway!' said Citrine, her eyes shining with excitement. 'Imagine, if the quake hadn't cracked the flagstone – we would never have found it.'

'Well,' said Folly, forgetting her irritation, her face for once suffused with astonishment, 'we have. And I say let's investigate.'

CHAPTER 7

SUBTERRANEAN PEREGRINATIONS

Folly went first, swinging her legs over the edge of the hole and lowering herself down.

'It's not a long drop,' she called up. 'Hand me my light.'

Vincent passed down the lantern and Folly held it out in front of her. 'I'm in a tunnel,' she said. Her echoing voice was eerily distorted.

Vincent followed eagerly, his shining smitelight picking out Folly's figure ahead of him. Jonah waited for Citrine, who was collecting her Klepteffigium, and allowed her to go before him. He had a little trouble squeezing through the space, but was relieved to find that it was slightly wider than he had feared.

The four now stood in a rocky passageway with curved walls and a flattened floor. The ceiling was high enough for them to walk upright, even Jonah. The air was cool but not stale, and there was a definite breeze blowing in the direction of the Kryptos. The floor consisted of a mixture of gravel and damp, sandy earth. The only noise was the sound of

the steady *drip, drip, drip* of water. Here and there the walls glistened wetly.

The party made good progress along the tunnel's gentle slope. Folly was striding ahead purposefully. Vincent was keeping up with her, partly because with Citrine and Jonah side by side there was no room for a third person. They were lagging because Citrine kept stopping to use the Klepteffigium.

Jonah was intrigued. 'How exactly does that . . . thing work?' he asked.

Citrine handed him the small brown box and showed him where to insert a piece of stiff Depiction paper into a narrow slot at the back. 'You look through here,' she said, 'and line up what you want to capture within the frame. If they're too far away or too close, just wind the proximus handle. Then, to take the Depiction, push up this toggle switch and stand steady. After a few seconds you'll see a flash and hear a click.'

Jonah took the contraption and looked through the small eyehole. His large hands almost covered the box. The lens distorted the figures up the tunnel, swelling them in the middle and thinning them out at top and bottom. He made adjustments as Folly had explained, and framed Citrine and Vincent with a generous margin. Then, satisfied with his composition, he flicked the switch. There was a bright flash, he waited for the click and handed the box back to Citrine.

'Simple,' she said with a smile.

'But where's the Depiction?'

'On the paper inside,' said Citrine, 'but I need some chemicals to finish it. They're in my bedroom. I wish I had thought to take them last time I was in the house.'

'What about Wenceslas?' suggested Jonah. 'He has all sorts in the Caveat Emptorium – he might sell you some.'

Citrine's face brightened. 'Of course!' and the two continued, taking turns with the gadget as they went.

Further up the tunnel, hoping that Folly was no longer cross with him, Vincent had fallen into step beside her. 'So, where do you think this leads?'

'Presumably the slab was a way out for Lady Degringolade if she awoke from the dead,' said Folly, and when Vincent looked sceptical she added with a grin, 'We *are* in Degringolade.'

Vincent knew then that he had been forgiven for his earlier behaviour. He looked over his shoulder at Jonah and Citrine. 'Thick as thieves, those two,' he said cheerfully, 'even though they come from very different worlds.'

'Do you think we have more in common?'

Vincent made a rocking motion with his head to indicate that he wasn't sure either way, earning a rare laugh from Folly.

The tunnel turned unexpectedly, widening out into a

small chamber with three other exits.

'It's a crossroads,' said Vincent, and started patting his many pockets. Finally he produced a compass, but regardless of which way he turned it the needle just kept spinning. 'It must be that stuff you told me about, the magnetic ore under the marsh.' And to prove it he flicked the magnetic switch on his wrist. 'There's a very strong pull down here.'

'You're right – impedimentium,' said Folly. 'You can see it.' She pointed to long copper-coloured streaks that ran across the chamber walls like glittering veins. Scattered about the ground there were pebbles of the same colour, varying in size.

Vincent pocketed a few of them and noticed at the same time that there were markings etched into the centre of the chamber floor. 'Compass points,' he said in surprise.

Folly looked where he was pointing. North, south, east and west were clearly marked, each pointing to one of the exits. 'Could be useful,' she remarked. They had come from the south, she noted, as she sat on a broad ledge near the north exit. She took out her Blivet and started to wipe it clean with a rag from her satchel. 'We should wait for the others.'

'Did you use that to kill the Pluribus?' asked Vincent, sitting beside her. He smiled inwardly at the question. Eminently practical, his father's son, he had never imagined words like Pluribus would trip off his tongue so easily, as if he had known them all his life. He had not intended to stay so long in Degringolade, but when Folly had called his bluff he'd realized he wasn't so sure he wanted to leave after all. Apart from the fact that he didn't want to travel through Antithica in the coldness of Gevra, he had to admit, though begrudgingly, that he was beginning to enjoy the company of the others. Like Citrine, he also wanted to find out more about Folly's past.

'I didn't really kill it,' she was saying. 'The Blivet disperses things like that, but it doesn't get rid of them. You can't ever get rid of Superents completely – they will always exist in one form or another. They're all made up of Supermundane particles, but some have more sticking power than others, I suppose. You could say the Blivet neutralizes them. It's temporary, though some stay neutralized longer than others.'

She gave the now gleaming tines another careful sweep of the cloth. Beautifully crafted and strange to behold, it was hard to believe the Blivet was a weapon. It was more like some sort of tool. Folly held it up to examine it with a critical dark-blue eye and just for that instant Vincent saw her in a completely different light. Now she really did look like the Supermundane hunter she claimed to be. Her hair, white-blonde, had dried slicked back, and her mouth was set in a determined line. The hood of her leather coat framed her pale face and the angle of her jaw gave her an air of grim resolve.

Vincent thought he understood why she was so upset about his recklessness. Everything that had happened to him since he had come to Degringolade – the danger, the close escapes, Kamptulicon – it was all an adventure for him, but for Folly it was a way of life. He should respect it.

'Have you another?' he blurted out.

Folly's head jerked, taken aback by the question. 'You want a Blivet?'

Vincent suddenly felt a little embarrassed by his request. 'You never know when it might come in handy,' he mumbled.

'Traditionally they're passed down within families, from one Supermundane hunter to another. This belonged to my great-great-grandmother.'

'What about your father? He must have had one.'

Folly hesitated. 'It was lost when he died.'

Vincent thought for a moment. 'And Axel?'

Folly looked at him coolly. 'Yes, he had one, but I don't know where that is either.'

Vincent broke the awkward silence. 'Where do you think that Pluribus came from?'

'Don't worry, we should be safe here,' said Folly, second-guessing him. 'Superents avoid places like this, crossroads, because they can be summoned here against their will.'

'Oh.' Vincent changed the subject. 'So anyway, you should have seen the look on Leucer's face in the wine merchant's.'

Folly's face darkened and Vincent oathed silently at his stupidity. He held up his hands in a conciliatory gesture. 'I know, it *was* stupid to be seen, but honestly, I was out of there before they knew what had happened.' A white lie, but it seemed to work and Folly visibly relaxed.

'I suppose there's no harm done really,' she admitted generously. 'I'm sorry if I have been a bit . . . stern. I haven't quite recovered from that whole business with Axel. Vincent, have you ever thought what *would* happen if you were caught? I mean, would you expect us to rescue you?'

'There's no cell can keep me. I can open any lock, believe me!'

Folly was no longer paying attention and the Blivet hung loosely in her hand. She was sitting very still, rigid almost, and her pale face was distinctly grey.

'Folly?' he said quietly. 'Are you all right?' He looked into her face and was unnerved to see that her eyes were fixed and staring, the pupils huge and black, almost engulfing her indigo irises. She seemed to be listening to something, but the chamber was silent. If Vincent didn't know better, he would have said that someone had hypnotized her. He was relieved when she stirred and came back to life. She looked briefly confused and gave him a terse smile.

'Just tired,' she said, and before he could enquire further a shadow darkened the floor.

'Codfish! What a great room!' declared Jonah, his huge frame filling the entrance. 'I could live here quite happily. Of course, the Kryptos is wonderful,' he added hurriedly, 'but sometimes it feels as small as a mermaid's purse.'

Citrine looked down one of the other tunnels. 'Which one shall we take? I'm intrigued as to where we'll end up.'

'Let's go north,' suggested Folly, getting to her feet as if nothing had happened. She was gone before anyone could object.

The northern passageway was similar to the one they had already travelled, but shortly after they entered it began to slope quite sharply upward.

'Hey, my compass is working again,' said Vincent.

'It smells a little fresher here too,' observed Citrine, but to everyone's disappointment at the next bend the tunnel came to an abrupt and rocky end.

'Well, that's that then,' said Jonah, unable to hide his relief. 'We'll have to go back.'

Folly came up behind him and pointed to the wooden trapdoor in the roof directly above his head. Admittedly it wasn't immediately obvious, and Jonah gave a resigned shrug. He was tall enough to reach it and pushed hard with the flat of his hands, but it didn't give. Then Vincent noticed a keyhole and so Jonah hoisted him on to his shoulders from where, rather awkwardly, Vincent picked the lock. The hatch was still stuck, however, so Jonah pushed harder and it gave suddenly, slamming noisily down on the floor above. Jonah gave Vincent a leg-up through the opening.

'Careful,' warned Citrine behind him. 'Knowing the Degringolades, there could be anything up there.'

Like what? wondered Vincent, then said aloud, 'It's some sort of storeroom. Do you think we've reached the city?'

Folly's face creased with a knowing smile. 'Not the city; *Degringolade Manor*!'

CHAPTER 8

DECREPITUDE

Vincent could hear Citrine protesting below as he stood and surveyed his new surroundings. His initial excitement waned somewhat when nothing of any great interest was revealed. He was in a larder to be precise, but it had an air of long abandonment, smelling of mildew and dead mice and decay. It was patently obvious that not a soul had set foot in the place for years. It was now the domain of spiders which, unhindered by humans, had patiently spun their thick sticky webs from point to point across the room and back again. A rat circumspectly emerged from behind a bag on a low shelf and then quite brazenly stood on its hind legs and eyed the intruder. Vincent shivered. Rodents made his flesh crawl.

Behind him his companions climbed up through the hole (using Jonah as a stepping stone) and the air became thick with the dust raised by the newcomers' feet. Citrine was holding her hand over her mouth to avoid inhaling it. 'We must be the first people in here for years.'

'You mean decades,' mumbled Jonah through his collar,

once he had hoisted himself up to join the others.

Citrine noted that this larder was significantly larger than the one in the Capodel Townhouse. It was cool, as was to be expected given its purpose, and there was a small window, high up in the wall, though no light came through its opaque pane. From a ladder-like frame attached to the ceiling there hung an array of copper pots and pans. The deep slate shelves were still laden with food containers, tins and cartons and bags, their contents mainly unidentifiable and shredded by mice. On a large tarnished platter sat the skull of a hog and on the floor beneath the shelves there were sacks of grain and flour and sugar, once full but now deflated and rotting away.

'Could be useful stuff here,' said Folly, eying the pots.

'Later.' Vincent was impatient to get going. He could think of far more useful things than pots to take away from a house this size. 'Let's explore.'

'Maybe we should we stay together,' suggested Citrine, 'for safety.'

Vincent scoffed loudly. 'There's nanyone here. The place is derelict.' He led them out of the larder and through the kitchen, between the wide food-preparation counters, past the dusty grey range oven, now cold but once the warm heart of the house, and up to the ground floor.

In its day Degringolade Manor had been the finest dwelling for miles. Even in its current dilapidated state it

still had a certain grandeur that instilled a sense of quiet awe in the four explorers. The entrance hall was of enormous proportions with a vaulted ceiling that seemed a hundred feet above. Despite the dirt, it was possible, just, to see the painted mosaics on the coffered panels. An enormous multi-tiered chandelier hung from a central rose, surrounded on three sides by the galleried landing. Jonah, never having seen such a sight, began to count the candles, but gave up after three score and five. Tiny crystals strung on chains dangled from the chandelier hoops, but they no longer sparkled. As with everything, the pendulous centrepiece looked as if someone had sprinkled it first with fine dust and then cast a net of gossamer cobwebs over it.

Vincent, like a bee to honey (like a flesh-fly to rotting meat, thought Jonah), presented himself before a gilded, flaking mirror hanging over a table against the wall. He rubbed it clean, but when he caught sight of the arch-browed expression on Folly's face behind him he quickly moved away. 'What exactly happened here?' he asked. 'Why is nobody living in this place?'

Citrine, the only true native of Degringolade, told them what she knew: how the sea had slowly flooded the Degringolade estate and created the salt marsh; how the ancient Degringolade family had had a run of bad luck and died, one after the other, until fifty years ago only Lord

Cornelius Degringolade was left. Without even a distant cousin left to marry, he had struggled to find a bride. The Degringolades were rich, but were now believed to be cursed. Cornelius was rumoured to be a hunchback, and to the city folk this was simply further proof of the blight upon them. Finally, against all previous tradition, he had settled on a woman from a noble yet unknown family somewhere in Antithica province. From the start, things had not augured well for the union. Within a year, with no heirs, the couple had become reclusive and were rarely seen again. Servants' jobs were short-lived, and they returned to the city with elaborate tales of the eccentricities of the lord and lady of the manor, especially Lady Scarletta.

'My father told me,' said Citrine, lowering her voice, 'that she used to throw servants who displeased her into the Tar Pit. The last servant to work there was so frightened at what he saw that he lost the power of speech, so he wrote it all down in a journal, but it was lost. Apparently there are secret rooms all over the manor and the servants used to hear screams, but couldn't tell where they were coming from. Eventually no one would work there any more and the Degringolades stopped coming into the city and were never seen again. The only person who dared go to the manor was their solicitor, and he came back one day and said they were both dead. No one really cared. Some people think Lady

Degringolade murdered her husband and then gave herself up to the Supermundane.'

'Presumably that's when the d'Avidus family gained control of the Tar Pit,' suggested Folly.

Vincent looked thoughtful. 'If those are Lady Degringolade's bones in the Kryptos, then why isn't Lord Degringolade in there too? And who owns the manor now?'

Citrine shrugged. 'I only know what I told you, and that is what my father told me. I think eventually the house will pass to the city, a promise made by the first Degringolades. But with all the weird stories about Lady Scarletta, people stayed away because they were afraid and it was left to rot. Degringoladians don't like to tempt fate. They observe the rituals without question.'

'It's a wonder this place survived the earthquake,' said Jonah.

Citrine pulled on one of the curtains that were drawn over the window beside the solid wooden front door. The material ripped to shreds instantly and both the curtain and its heavy pole came crashing down. The noise was all the more shocking because of the contrasting silence of the manor. A huge cloud of smutty particles seemed to explode from the rotting, moth-eaten material, as indeed did a fluttering of moths. Citrine dissolved in a fit of coughing.

Vincent wiped a small patch of grubby windowpane and

looked out. It was dark outside, as much because nature had encroached so wholly upon the surroundings as from the depths of Nox itself. What had once been a broad, gravelled drive wide enough for a coach and four to turn in a graceful arc, was now a jungle of broad-leaved bushes. He thought he saw something move and pressed his nose against the cold glass, his hands shielding his face to avoid the reflection of the lights behind him. But whatever it was, or wasn't, had gone. He felt something hard underfoot and found he was standing on a three-legged frog made from finely sculpted adderstone. It must have been knocked from its perch on the door frame (placed there for luck in the Degringolade tradition) when the curtain came down. He pocketed it, naturally, and turned his attention to the rest of the house. He was not concerned with the decay that surrounded him, more with the things that might have survived the ravages of time and neglect, namely jewellery, gold, silver. Surely there was a chance they would still be here.

Together the four went from room to room and it was the same story in each one: Degringolade Manor was a study in magnificent decay and they were almost spellbound at the vestigial beauty of the huge rooms, each of them imagining what it must have been like when there was life within the walls, when fires burned brightly in the deep wide fireplaces and servants scurried along the corridors. There was little for

Vincent to salvage; everything was rotting away in the damp salty air.

'Maybe we could stay in the manor,' suggested Jonah to Citrine in the dining room. The table was still laid, as if at any moment someone was going to come in and sit down.

'Maybe,' murmured Citrine doubtfully, taking another Depiction. Every flash of the Klepteffigium was followed by the sounds of small creatures running away.

Vincent left them to their musings and followed Folly back to the hall. Together they climbed the marble staircase, a wide central installation with broad handrails and elaborate spindles. Ivy was carved decoratively into the wood, but if you looked closely enough you could see little impish creatures brazenly staring right back out at you. The carpet that ran up the middle of the stairs – originally a deep green – was held in place by similarly carved stair rods. It disintegrated beneath their feet.

Vincent examined the portraits that accompanied him as he ascended. By the looks of them, the Degringolade family were a dour lot, with deep-furrowed brows and a supercilious expression that had been passed down through the centuries. He brushed his hand across one canvas to remove the dust but drew it back sharply when a splinter from the frame lodged in his palm. He pulled it out and a droplet of blood swelled from the wound. He tied his handkerchief round his hand

and stood back to look at the portrait. Two leonine golden eyes stared out at him from a pale face, and the hint of a smile played on the woman's narrow lips. But there was cruelty in the smile. Vincent knew this had to be Lady Degringolade herself, the outsider in the family. She was sitting on a high-backed throne-like chair and looked for all the world like a regent. She was wearing a necklace and a browpin and her fingers were adorned with large rings. He thought of her dry bones in the Kryptos and could imagine quite vividly how she might have stalked with haughty pride these once sumptuous halls.

Folly had already reached the galleried landing and had walked away out of sight. He toyed with the idea of going after her, but he had his reasons not to, so decided to leave her to her own devices.

Having burgled plenty of large houses in his time, Vincent was familiar with the layout and reckoned that the main bedrooms and dressing rooms would be a good place to start. At the far end of the gallery there was a grand set of panelled double doors. With a degree of caution – his thieving instincts already to the fore – Vincent opened one door, tearing a large cobweb as he did so, and closed it softly behind him. He could tell immediately that the air in this room had not been disturbed for many years.

He pointed his light inside and illuminated an eerie sight.

He was in a bedroom furnished with a large four-poster bed, the dark curtains of which were drawn all around it. In the fireplace a fire was laid but unlit, the logs covered in thick smuts that had fallen down the chimney over the years. Upon closer inspection the rampant decay was evident here too. Moths fluttered up from beneath his feet at every step and jagged holes in the skirting revealed pairs of tiny glistening eyes.

Above the fire was a large painting. At first glance it looked like a still life, complete with fruit and flowers, but as Vincent stared he saw that it was not a representation of life, more of decline and death. The fruit was rotting and crawling with flies, the flowers wilting, the candles burned down and the snuffer lying on the table. Half hidden under a dead leaf was a broken timepiece, and staring out from behind the vase was a leering skull on a plate. This was a vanitas painting, a reminder to the viewer of the transience of life.

Grimacing, Vincent turned away and his smitelight's beam fell upon a dark archway in the other wall.

'Aha!' he exclaimed. 'The dressing room.' He passed beneath the arch through a short hallway into an ante-room where the air was so heavy he felt it pressing down on his chest. His practised burglar's eye took in a large dressing table with a central mirror between two smaller ones. The black cloth across the mirrors had rotted away.

Laid out on the dresser top was a set of ivory-handled hairbrushes and an array of perfume bottles and pots. At the edge a pair of slim china hands for holding jewellery stood side by side, but the fingers were ringless and no chains hung from the necklace tree.

He picked up, examined and discarded most of the objects. The perfume bottles were empty, their contents having evaporated over the years, except for one, a brown bottle in the shape of a pear, which still had liquid in it so he took it. He also took an oval silver compact. It could be worth something. He flicked open the lid, releasing a cloud of powder, and a soft sponge fell out and disintegrated. He was surprised to find that the interior of the compact glowed, as if it had its own source of light. He saw his reflection in the mirrored lid, just his eyes and the bridge of his nose, but it was blurry so he snapped the lid shut and dropped it into a pocket.

He took, for the Kryptos, a hand-held mirror to replace the one which had broken. Despite Folly's apparent disdain for such things, he had seen her glance in the mirror more than once and he knew Citrine liked to adjust her hair. Jonah, with his livid scars, was the only one who was not interested in seeing his reflection

Next Vincent started on the drawers, which one by one crumbled away in his hand. He came across some rectangular

velvet-lidded boxes and was delighted to find inside pearls and brooches. In another he found a set of earrings and a matching necklace, and in the third he scooped up a selection of rings.

Satisfied with his haul, though it was relatively meagre for a place such as this, Vincent made ready to go. The disturbed air was becoming unpleasantly gritty in his throat.

With one final sweep of the smitelight he caught sight of an embroidered three-panelled screen. He peeked behind it and was faced with a black cloth on the wall.

'Another mirror,' he mused, and pulled away the fragile cloth. The looking glass behind it was large with candle-holders incorporated into either side of the gilded frame. Where he might have expected to see fat-cheeked cherubs (he had come across plenty of ornate mirrors in his career) there were instead more of the impish creatures he had glimpsed on the stairs.

His smitelight was shining directly on the glass, but there was something odd about his reflection. It was as if he wasn't properly there. He went closer, and tapped across the mirror from one edge to the other.

'Domne!' he breathed. 'I think there is something on the other side.' He fumbled around the frame for a latch or a button – snapping one of the candle-holders in the process – anything that might prove his theory correct, but it was only when he pressed on one of the hands of a beckoning imp that there was an almost imperceptible click and the mirror opened outwards like a door. Making sure to wedge it open – Vincent knew better than to take the chance that it might close behind him – he pointed his smitelight into the space and stepped through.

His heart stuttered. 'Spletivus,' he whispered. His mouth went suddenly dry and an overwhelming sense of déjà-vu swamped him. 'What in Aether is this?'

Chapter 9

On the Other Side of the Looking Glass

For a split second Vincent was transported back to Leopold Kamptulicon's hideous Ergastirion, the secret cellar where he had been trapped and tortured and had ultimately lost the fingers of his right hand. Quickly he pulled himself together, though the shock of the memory had sent an unpleasant thrill through his veins. He breathed deeply and took stock of his surroundings.

He was in a small cavern-like room, unnervingly similar to the Cunningman's. He recognized with horror the wicked paraphernalia picked out by the beam of his smitelight – the goat skulls, the leathery wings, the peacock feathers, the pickled shapes in the jars – only this time there was more of it. The passage of years had not detracted from its hideous presentation, but made it even more ghastly, and he was not inured to it, not by a long chalk.

He directed his light away from the apothecary bottles, the contents of which were *not* for healing, and focused instead on the circular table to his right. The rotting folds of the cover hung limply from the edge. In the middle there was a half-burnt candle and next to it a deck of cards, like Citrine's. Someone had been card-spreading.

Vincent went closer, his nerves jangling, picked up the deck and shuffled the cards. They were a different design to Citrine's, and the flavour of the deck was unpleasant; the character cards wore expressions of loathing and malice, and some of the more grotesque images were difficult to stomach. Also on the table were the four accompanying pieces of maerl. Vincent jiggled three in the palm of his hand, then decisively tumbled them across the table as he had seen Citrine do. But he did not know what came next so he just gathered everything up, cards and maerl, and dropped it into a well-preserved leather bag that was lying on a nearby stool.

Vincent began to walk slowly round the curved perimeter of the room. He thought he must be in a tower, for there were no corners. Then something crunched under his foot. It looked as if someone had sprinkled Natron across the floor. The room was cool, but Vincent was sweating. Slowly he lifted his smitelight and shone it into the dark centre. He saw sturdy treen legs, the claw-and-ball feet, the metal plates that bolted them to the floor. The light moved upward, revealing now the ornately carved rigid back and the two round ears on either side.

To many this was just a chair. But to Vincent it was

something he had only seen once before and had hoped to never see again.

A Sella Subjunctum.

Folly had told him its name. He had thought of it only as a chair of torture. It was in a chair such as this, at the hands of Leopold Kamptulicon, that he had been restrained and maimed and had feared his life would end. And now here was another one in Degringolade Manor. Unwillingly, yet unable to stop himself, Vincent rounded the chilling seat. He swore under his breath and a wave of nausea washed over him. But no longer was it the sight of the chair that caused such revulsion.

It was the mummified body that was strapped into it.

Brown, wrinkled and desiccated, the body sat strangely upright, staring straight ahead, grinning insanely. It was held tightly at the neck, just as he had been in Kamptulicon's secret cellar, and its legs were strapped at the ankles. When he had composed himself enough to look closer, he deduced from the tattered clothes that this dried-up leathery figure had once been a woman.

He couldn't help but imagine this poor wretch's last hours, for there was no doubt in his mind that she had met her end in this chair. Perhaps at the hands of Lord and Lady Degringolade. Or maybe it was Kamptulicon who had conducted the terror, as he had once tortured Vincent. He dismissed the thought – Kamptulicon was a recent visitor to Degringolade and this must have happened a long time ago.

Vincent took the amulet that hung round the shrivelled neck and the ring from one of the dried-up fingers. It felt loose, but it would not come off easily, and he ended up breaking the finger at the knuckle. Something glittered on the mummy's brow, and, never one to be squeamish when it came to money, Vincent pulled out a browpin with its dulled precious stone. The brown skin stretched as he did so and the skull came forward and then fell back against the chair with a bang. Vincent jumped and froze, but nothing untoward ensued so he continued to inspect his finding. The underside of the browpin was inscribed 'Decus et tutanem', and he made a note to ask Folly the meaning of the words.

He noticed that in the course of retrieving the pin he had managed to smear blood from his wounded hand across the mummy's forehead. He shuddered, slightly repulsed at his own actions. It was time to leave the macabre scene.

Closing the mirror-door behind him, Vincent stood in the dressing room and listened. He thought he heard the others calling his name. He hurried back to the bedroom. Was it his imagination or had the room become very cold? He licked his lips; there was a strange metallic taste in his mouth. He could feel something vibrating on the air, as if someone was humming. He exhaled through chattering teeth and his

breath clouded in front of him. Now his hands were tingling with the chill and he had the feeling he was no longer alone. He shone his smitelight all around the room and then back to the curtained bed. Was there something on the other side of the curtains?

The curtain moved and he saw it, a huge shape, glowing green, the like of which he had never imagined in his life, manifesting itself by the bed.

'Domne!' he hissed. He dug his hand into his pocket, brought out a fistful of black beans and flung them directly at the . . . thing. He didn't know what else to call it. The beans made no difference, merely passing into its mucilaginous folds with a soft swallowing sound. He backed slowly towards the door through which he had first entered the room. He fired the Natron disperser, showering the creature with the repellent salt. He thought it might have flinched, but then it was moving towards him. He let out a roar of terror before fleeing the room.

Tripping and skidding out on to the gallery, Vincent raced towards the stairs. Citrine and Jonah, who were on their way up, called out to him, but at the sight of his pursuer they stopped in their tracks, then turned as one and fled back down. Vincent reached the top of the stairs and looked over his shoulder. The thing was right behind him. He felt it touch his arm and his skin burned through his sleeve.

He opened his mouth to scream, when from out of nowhere Folly came running towards him. 'Keep your mouth shut!' she shouted. 'Protect your face.'

Crushed by a terrible weight on his back, Vincent dropped to his knees and curled up as tightly as possible. He was sure that he was only seconds from death. He was vaguely aware of footsteps to his left, and then a plunging sound, like a stone dropping into soft mud

There was a roar of such magnitude that the ground shook. For a moment he thought it was another earthquake and wondered if the house could possibly stand it. Icy wetness drenched him, and when he dared to open his eyes he saw to his disgust that he was sitting in the middle of a pool of what could only be described as cold slime. He rolled up slowly to a kneeling position. Strings of the green goo stretched between his fingers. Folly was in front of him, holding out a cloth. 'Wipe your face,' she said. 'Before the ghouze gets in your eyes or mouth or up your nose. It'll make you ill.'

Vincent took the cloth and cleaned his face. Shaking, he got to his feet. 'What the Hades was that?'

'*That* was a Pluribus,' said Folly grimly.

'I thought you said you blivved it,' he gasped, still catching his breath.

'It must be another one.'

'Two? In one day?'

‘Exactly,’ said Folly. ‘It’s not a good sign. It’s time to get out of here.’

Together they hurried downstairs. Folly, at Vincent’s side, allowed herself a short burst of laughter. ‘Blivved it,’ she said. ‘I’ve never heard it called that before.’

Citrine and Jonah were waiting at the bottom, very apologetic about their cowardice, but Folly praised them for their good instincts. ‘You don’t hang around when a Pluribus is on the loose,’ she said. Citrine fussed over Vincent, cleaning off remnants of slime with her pocket handkerchief, and for once he didn’t object. Jonah went to pat him on the back, but stopped in mid-air when he noticed the ghouze.

‘There’s something you should both see,’ Vincent said, and went to the window by the main door. Folly, tuning in to his unusually serious tone, hurried across and peered out. Her face remained expressionless. A single Pluribus, palpitating, like a still-beating heart plucked from the chest, was standing just feet from the glass.

‘We really have to go,’ said Folly firmly. Jonah pulled on her arm and pointed slightly to one side, where there stood a dozen or more of the creatures. Degringolade Manor was surrounded by a horde of shivering Pluriba.

‘So, now can I have a Blivet?’ asked Vincent.

Chapter 10

From the *Degringolade Daily*

Earthquake Rocks Degringolade!

Reported by Hepatic Whitlock

Last night, just before Mid-Nox, in an unusual twist of geological fate, this great city of Degringolade was shaken to its core by an earthquake! It is believed at this time that it originated somewhere on the outskirts of the city and lasted almost thirty seconds. A few minor aftershocks have since been reported, but experts say that the likelihood of another major event is remote. The last recorded earthquake in Degringolade took place over two centuries ago. Historically the province of Antithica is not prone to seismic shifts at all.

It has been posited that the recent inferno at the d'Avidus Tar Pit might have brought about the earthquake, but this has been dismissed. Dr Winthrop Rayleigh, on a serendipitous visit to Degringolade from the Antithica Institute of Geology, said, 'Seismic

shifts take place at great depths below the earth. There is no evidence anywhere that a trauma so close to the surface, unless it was a significant force, could bring on an actual earthquake. I am confident that the timing of this event so soon after the fire at the Tar Pit of Degringolade is nothing more than a coincidence.'

There were reports of unusual animal behaviour prior to the quake. People gave accounts of mice, rats and other small creatures running wildly through their houses. The large flock of gulls that nests on the rocks around the lighthouse was seen to be very disturbed and the lighthouse itself is now leaning and has been declared unsafe.

Unfortunately there has also been some structural damage around the city, generally to older brick buildings. Fortunately the funicular railway that runs up to the Governor's Residence at the summit of Collis Hill came through unscathed, much to Governor d'Avidus's relief.

It has also been reported, though not confirmed, that the contents of a warehouse at the Capodel Manufactory were destroyed. Edgar Capodel, owner of the Capodel Chemical Company, has assured this newspaper that no chemical containers were damaged in the earthquake and that all such equipment and stocks are kept in secure conditions. Rumours abound that Mr Capodel is developing a food cooling system at the factory, but this is a story that Mr Capodel will neither confirm nor deny.

Chief Guardsman Fessup has warned citizens to be on the lookout for looters and in particular to be alert for any member of the so-called 'Phenomenals' gang, who might well seek to take advantage of the chaos in the aftermath of the earthquake to commit their trademark criminal acts.

In addition to all this upset, the Kronometer in Mercator Square has stopped working. It is thought that this is the first time the clock has stopped in its two-hundred-year existence. It was last wound thirteen days ago, in line with the lunar cycle. The clock was commissioned and donated to the city by Lord Barnaby Degringolade, a many times great-grandfather of Lord Cornelius Degringolade, the last inhabitant of Degringolade Manor, whose death, along with that of his wife, Lady Scarletta, in mysterious circumstances over fifty years ago, brought the Degringolade bloodline to an end.

The Kronometer's stopping reminds us all of the prophecy engraved on the clock's pendulum:

Should ere this pendulum of blackened brass,
No longer swing its graceful pass,
Beware the risen Degringolade
For blood will smear their sharpened blade!

It goes without saying that the city's engineers are working all hours in an effort to restart the Kronometer. They report that their efforts are hampered by the numerous tokens offered to the Supermundane already affixed to the thirteen pillars by concerned Degringoladians since the fire. Governor d'Avidus has stated that although he understands the reason for the tokens, and how important it is to placate Supermundane entities in times of upset, he would beseech the citizens to desist from hanging any more until the Kronometer is repaired.

CHAPTER 11

A MEETING OF MINDS

Leucer d'Avidus, the serving Governor of Degringolade, grunted and dropped the creased newspaper on the floor beside him. He settled again in the leather wingback chair by the fire in Edgar Capodel's study.

'I don't believe in coincidences,' he said, shooting a dark and meaningful look at Leopold Kamptulicon, who was standing at the hearth.

The Cunningman took the bait. 'What! You think the earthquake is my fault?'

'Who's to say that your failure at the Tar Pit didn't have something to do with it? Geologists and seismologists, or whatever they are called, aren't known for their expertise in the Supermundane.'

Kamptulicon was not in a good mood. He was still recovering from his own experience of the earthquake. He had had to walk a half-mile to catch up with his horse, and his ongoing ever-present resentments were closer than usual to the surface.

'Domne, Leucer, no one could have predicted what happened at the Tar Pit. That girl and her thieving friend wrecked it all. I risked my life for you, and for what?'

Leucer snorted. 'If anyone was at risk at the Tar Pit, I believe it was I, dear fellow. You, as I recall, weren't even there until it was almost over. Let me think . . . oh yes, you were trying to capture those domnable Phenomenals. And you failed at that too.'

Kamptulicon was on the verge of an apoplectic fit. 'It was Fessup's guards who let them go –'

Leucer waved his hand dismissively. 'Excuses, excuses. I suppose you blame them for the loss of your Omnia Intum as well.'

Kamptulicon made a sharp sound of vexation. He pointed his finger at Leucer and his ring sparkled in the firelight. 'I might not have my book, but I have other tricks up my sleeve.'

Leucer laughed. 'Are you threatening me?'

'Just warning you, I'm not your lackey.'

'Well, that is debatable.'

The door opened and Edgar came in carrying a tray of drinks. The feuding pair broke off. Kamptulicon's brows were knitted angrily but Leucer, a natural politician, pasted a benign smile on his face. Nevertheless, the hostility in the room was palpable.

Edgar tutted. 'Gentlemen, please, enough of these

quarrels. What is it between you two?'

Edgar had gleaned quite early on that if either of them had his way Kamptulicon and Leucer would each never see the other again. For the time being, however, they were just about able to put aside their differences and maintain a show of civilityas long as necessity demanded it.

'I see you are surviving without your servants,' said Leucer, picking casually at the knees of his trousers.

'Oh yes,' said Edgar breezily. 'I hardly miss them – always skulking about and eavesdropping.'

'You can't be too careful, I suppose, but it's hardly fitting for a man of your status to have no servants. That in itself might arouse suspicion.'

'A girl comes in for a couple of hours every day and does what needs to be done. I eat at the Bonchance Club at night. Excellent food, as you know.'

Edgar offered round the drinks – vintage crystal-clear chilled Grainwine – leaned his walking stick against the wall (the stick was an affectation if truth be told; his leg had healed well after the incident with the Trikuklos at the gallows, but he rather liked playing the invalid, and the ladies rather liked it too) and propped an elbow on the mantelpiece to warm himself by the fire.

Outside, the sleet that had been slapping wetly against the window was turning to snow; Gevra was harsh in Antithica

province, and the approaching thirteenth month the harshest. Over the coming weeks Degringolade's steel rooftops and copper domes would be concealed under a thick white counterpane. Edgar swirled his drink in the glass and slicked back a stray lock of hair that was brushing his forehead. The firelight overemphasized his dark good looks to the extent that he almost became a caricature of himself. He *tsk*ed and gestured at the newspaper on the floor. 'You see, Leucer, that the *Degringolade Daily* got the news about the warehouse? I didn't speak to them. No doubt Hepatic Whitlock persuaded one of my loyal workers to.'

'What state are they in, my order of special Cold Cabinets?'

'Damaged by the earthquake, though not beyond repair. It will take time. I only have a few workers on the job, the ones I can trust.'

Leucer smiled broadly. 'Imagine it! With the help of those cabinets I, and you of course, will have a workforce that never tires, answers back or makes unreasonable demands. An industrialist's dream.' He shrugged. 'So, for now, I can wait. Besides, it would be prudent to let the dust settle over that Tar Pit incident first. It's still the talk of the taverns. Everyone is in a state of hysteria about Lurids and Superents and Domne knows what. What the people want more than anything is the capture of these brass-necked toerags.' He frowned and sloshed a mouthful of Grainwine noisily between his teeth.

'And the sooner the better. I didn't become governor to deal with common vandals. I have far more important matters to attend to. Professor Soanso will be here in a couple of days.'

'Who?' Kamptulicon was only half listening, still ruminating on his own problems.

Edgar, who had been regularly checking the time and peering out between the parted curtains, looked up at the mention of the professor. 'Arkwright Soanso,' he said. 'Surely you have heard of him? The famous scientist who discovered kekrimpari. Hubert was always talking about it – he said it could be another source of energy at the manufactory.'

'It's all part of the greater plan,' explained Leucer impatiently. 'I reckon this kekrimpari could be used with the Lurids, when we have them. Professor Soanso is doing a demonstration at the Degringolade Playhouse. Everyone will be there.'

'Speaking of plans,' said Edgar, 'if we want to catch the Phenomenals, we have to draw them out, on our terms. Get one, the others will follow. We've enough on them now to throw them all in the penitentiary and toss the key.' A loud clatter at the door made them all jump. 'And speaking of keys, my visitor has arrived.'

Edgar left the room and returned shortly with a man of dubious-looking appearance (and, it was quickly established, character). He was short and sinewy, with big dirty hands and

one of those faces that are most often described as 'shifty'. The black grime under his fingernails and the faint odour of metal that hung about him caused Leucer to grimace and sniff. The man smiled crookedly, revealing an odd assortment of teeth. He doffed his cap defiantly rather than deferentially and spoke stridently with a strong Degringoladian accent, admittedly that of the lower classes.

'Gud evun, gennerlmen, Quinque Boughton at yore servus.'

He pronounced his name with a hard *q*, in the classical way, and the *gh* was like an *f*, so he actually said 'Kinky Bofton'.

'I bin tolled yews are having trubble with a certain young Vincent Verdigris.'

Leucer looked at the man through narrowed eyes. 'And what if we are?'

Quinque moved his own eyebrows rapidly, a habit that lent an air of conspiracy to whatever he said. 'Some years ago I wus travellin', as yer do, when I came across a group of fellers deep in the Antithican Peaks. A contest was underway, and the challenge wus to open a lock that was deemed unbreakable. I watched 'em come and fail and go, but then, when the day was nearly done and the lock near declared impossible, this feller stepped out of the crowd and within moments he had it picked and the safe door open. There wus a boy with him, and all the while he was begging his father to give him a go. To cut a long story short –' Quinque's attentive audience looked somewhat relieved at this – 'the man's name was Linus Verdigris.'

'Verdigris?' Kamptulicon's eyes widened and he leaned forward. 'Vincent's father!'

Leucer too was now listening intently, turning his gold ring round and round on his finger, setting aside his revulsion and scepticism.

Edgar had folded his arms and was looking particularly smug. 'It struck me that young Vincent might be just like his father, *unable to resist a challenge*.'

Leucer was already one step ahead of him. 'Then a challenge he shall have.'

Chapter 12
The Awakening

Nox blanketed Degringolade greedily, spreading itself across the city, no corner or alley or doorway out of its tenebrous reach. Degringoladians, having worked all day and dined on horsemeat pie and supped glasses of ale and read the paper and dozed by the fire, roused themselves from their chairs and made their weary way to bed. Some stopped a moment on the stair to listen, pondering on the unusually loud wailing of the Lurids.

It was indeed loud. Down at the Tar Pit everything was very much awake.

The nebulous Lurids were flocked together in a shimmering crowd right in the middle of the unhallowed lake. They were all facing the same direction and howling in unison at the tops of their ghostly voices. A disturbance had started up under the inky surface. The tar rose but stayed intact, and whatever was beneath it travelled steadily towards the shore. The Lurids' moaning reached fever pitch as there emerged from under the tarry cloak a creature of great size and breadth.

By means of four huge legs it dragged itself out of the lake and stood on the shore, dripping tar and bones and whatever other detritus it had brought with it from the stinking depths. It spat and coughed and sneezed and lay down, exhausted, on the charred and bony shingle.

Katatherion was free.

Chapter 13
Triskaidekaphobia
Author's Note

'Triskaidekaphobia' is the fear of the number thirteen. Degringoladians, being so superstitious, always consider it an unlucky number. So, in keeping with Degringoladian tradition, there is no chapter thirteen in this book.

Chapter 14

When in Rome . . .

'Ow!' Vincent yelped and squirmed in his seat. Citrine, standing over him, grimaced and apologized. 'It's done,' she said. 'Look.' She held up the mirror from the manor so he could see her handiwork. Vincent looked at his reflection, specifically at the browpin that now pierced the soft flesh above his right eye.

'Where did you say you found this? In the dressing room? It might be one of Lady Degringolade's, you know.'

'I suppose it's possible,' he said lightly. *But highly unlikely*, he thought, with a surreptitious glance at the casket of bones. What Citrine didn't know was that he had pulled it from a mummy's brow. In fact, in his retelling of his discoveries in the manor, he had also omitted to mention the room behind the mirror. It wasn't that he was deliberately keeping it from them, but every time he started to say something about the dried-up body and the secret room he broke out in a sweat and felt nauseous. So he had glossed over it and tried to put it out of his mind. His brow was throbbing, despite the fact

that Citrine had numbed the area first with some ice from the Cold Cabinet wrapped in a cloth.

'Well, whoever owned it, they had excellent taste,' said Citrine. She had polished the stone and the silver pin until it shone, and secretly Vincent was very pleased with his new look.

'So, do you know,' he asked Folly, 'what the inscription means?'

'"*Decus et tutanem*"? Yes, I do. "An ornament and a safeguard". Sums up the purpose of a browpin, really. Fairly common in these parts.'

Jonah had watched the whole procedure with a wry smile. 'You're the last fellow I thought would do that. You laugh at Degringoladian superstition and now you're wearing a browpin.' He fingered his own earlobe and the protective earring he wore. Sailors favoured earrings over other jewellery.

'When in Degringolade . . .' said Citrine.

Vincent shrugged. 'I like it,' he said.. That much was true. He did like things that sparkled. But what he didn't say was how, ever since the Pluribus attack and the sight of such evilry in the manor, he was beginning to feel the need for such superstitious crutches. 'And who knows, maybe it will bring me luck.'

Folly examined the stone. 'Hmm, a sapphire. I don't know about luck, but it should afford you some protection.'

'From what?'

'From anything or any person who wishes you harm. It turns the evil against them.'

'That'll do. Though a Blivet would be even more useful.' Vincent handed back the mirror. 'Here, Citrine, I've got something for you.' He gave her the brown perfume bottle and she smiled.

'Why, kew, Vincent! I wonder how it has kept its smell.' She squeezed the bulb and inhaled the mist of scent.

And promptly fell to the floor in a swoon.

Jonah came to her side immediately and lifted her head, and Vincent fanned her with a copy of the *Degringolade Daily*.

Folly took the brown bottle and gave it a very cautious sniff at arm's length. She quickly replaced the lid and Vincent took it back.'This isn't perfume. This is narkos, a knockout potion. Domna, we're lucky the bottle didn't break. We'd all be asleep.'

'Will she be all right?' asked Jonah.

Folly nodded. 'She didn't inhale much. Give her twenty minutes. Your Lady Degringolade had a strange taste in scent.'

After the grand decay of Degringolade Manor, the Kryptos seemed even smaller than ever. The snow had not quite settled on the marsh, on account of the salt, but the ground

was hard and the watery pools were thick and slushy. The temperature in the Kryptos had dropped and the days the four companions had spent huddled around the fire, eating and drinking, seemed like weeks. Their physical appetites might have been satisfied, but mentally they were not at ease. The cracked slab was a constant reminder of what had happened in Degringolade Manor, and the malevolent host of Pluriba was very much at the forefront of their minds.

Vincent was sitting on his bedroll rubbing unguent into his scar. It was still swollen, but not such an angry red now, and he was gradually getting used to its appearance. Citrine, fully recovered from her brush with narkos earlier in the week, was examining the metal hand that Vincent had unscrewed from the arm piece. 'Is this the magnetic switch?' she asked.

Vincent nodded and there was a soft click as Citrine flicked it. Just then Folly offered her a bowl of slumgullion, so she passed the hand back to Vincent. He reached for it but she jerked it away from him. He tutted. He hadn't been feeling quite right since the visit to the manor and he wasn't in the mood for jokes.

'Citrine,' he said, 'just give me my hand.' He reached for it again, again she jerked it away and this time she dropped it and *it began to walk away on its fingers.*

The two of them stared at it dumbstruck. 'It's not me,' she said quickly. 'It did it all by itself.'

Now the others were looking. 'Vincent, what did you do with that impedimentium you took from the tunnel?' asked Folly suddenly.

'It's still in my pocket,' he said slowly, transfixed by the walking hand. In a flash he realized what she was getting at. 'Switch off the magnetism,' he ordered.

Citrine grabbed the hand as it passed her feet and flicked the switch. Instantly the hand came to a stop. Excitedly, Vincent took it and set it in front of him, arranging the five fingers like the legs of some sort of crawling creature. He dug into one of his many pockets and took out a pebble of the copper-coloured rock. He flicked the switch again and held out the pebble in the direction of the hand, as if taking aim. To everyone's astonishment, the hand began to walk slowly on its finger-legs away from him.

Jonah was the most affected. His mouth hung open for some seconds before he spoke. 'Well, by the seven seas, I never thought I'd see anything like that. It looks alive.'

The hand continued across the floor. Vincent moved the pebble and it changed direction. He did this a few times, sending it back and forth, right and left, before scooping it up, laughing. 'The impedimentium seems to work *against* the magnetic force. With a bit of practice, who knows how useful this little trick could be!'

Folly raised an eyebrow. 'Against a Pluribus?'

'I thought you said they were rare,' chipped in Jonah.

'They are. And when they do appear, it's usually alone. They're not like Phenomenals, who gather in groups.'

'So, nany for years, and then a whole load of Pluribuses all come at once. Strikes me as odd, don't you think?'

'Pluriba,' corrected Citrine without thinking, and then immediately flushed and apologized for her bad manners. But Jonah didn't care.

'So, what is to be done about them?' he asked. 'Will they just go away?'

'Why does anything have to be done at all?' asked Vincent, examining with a new-found respect his remarkable metal hand.

Folly breathed out heavily through her mouth and shook her head slowly. 'Nothing *has* to be done, but if *we* don't take action, they might well do something about us. It's not as if they have our best interests at heart. They are harbingers of danger and discord.'

'There must be a reason they're all at the manor. Maybe they'll just stay there.' Citrine was trying to sound hopeful.

'And maybe they won't. As long as they're about, every time we cross the salt marsh we could be in danger. Nany of us should leave the Kryptos without as many deterrents as possible, Natron and black beans at the very least. Jonah, perhaps we can adapt your spear—'

'Huh! Black beans and Natron were useless against the one I met,' interrupted Vincent. 'We need another Blivet.' He was returning to what was becoming a familiar theme. 'I would be happy to carry one.'

Citrine nodded. 'Yes! At least then we could have one between two.'

'Wenceslas might well have something like that,' suggested Jonah.

'Or Axel,' said Vincent quietly. 'He was hanged here in Degringolade. Presumably he had it when he was arrested.'

Citrine shook her head at Vincent. 'Reminding Folly of her brother's crimes . . . it's hurtful.'

Folly shrugged. 'He wasn't always bad,' she said. 'He chose his own path. And you're right. He probably did have his Blivet on him. But that doesn't really help us.'

'We could ask him about it.'

Instantly all heads turned towards Vincent. Citrine's eyes widened. 'You mean, summon him?'

Now they all looked at Folly. Her mouth was set in a straight line, her blue eyes giving nothing away.

'Don't we need a bone?' asked Citrine nervously.

'I thought the Mangledore contained the only remaining bones of Axel, and I chucked that into the Tar Pit.' Jonah was not in any way pleased at the prospect of more Lurid-raising.

'Well, that's a . . . shame.' Citrine was barely able to hide her own relief.

Jonah yawned loudly and stretched. 'Pluriba or no, it's late. I'm off to bed.'

That seemed to put paid to any more conversation about Axel and his Blivet and the others followed Jonah's lead. Vincent, from his own bed, watched through slitted eyes as Folly tended the fire before settling herself under her blankets with the book. It was rarely out of her sight. He sensed, as he had done these last few nights, that for some reason she was waiting for everyone to go to sleep.

He closed his eyes and allowed his mind to wander. He used to love that time between wakefulness and sleep. His father had told him many years ago of the Hypnagogue and the Hypnopomp; the first led you into slumber and the second led you out. He had thought they were characters in a fairy tale, but now, as he immersed himself more and more in the life and lore of Degringolade, he wondered if perhaps they really did exist. He could feel himself drifting off and remembered how this adventure had started: how he had been left at the border of Antithica province and had his first sight of Degringolade's adamantine roofs glittering in the morning sun. Now it was the snow that glittered.

A face came floating in front of his eyes, a woman's face, and he shook his head to make it go away. But the vision remained. He had seen the face before, in recent dreams, and he knew those golden eyes, but think as he might he just couldn't place who it was. He tried to look closer, but now he was too far gone towards sleep, his muscles paralysed. She was saying something but he couldn't hear, he could only see the white edge of her teeth on her lower lip as she shaped a *v* with her mouth.

Chapter 15

Family Reunion

Vincent wasn't sure what woke him. Perhaps a log shifting on the fire, or maybe the ever-present howling of the Lurids expressing indignation at their plight. It wasn't the Kronometer's bell, which remained silent, or the clanking of the funicular railway. More likely it was his scar, which was throbbing, and he debated taking another slug of Antikamnial. He sighed. He was trying to cut down on it. Folly had warned him against taking too much. It wasn't that it was harmful per se, but it did have side effects and could become addictive, which led to a whole other set of problems. Vincent was confident that he could do without it, but he also knew that it would take the edge off the pain.

He looked to where Folly slept. Her voluble sleep-mutterings had disturbed him more than once these last few nights. But she lay in a dark unmoving shape under her blankets, blankets he had stolen for the Kryptos.

Light and heat came from the dying fire, but he was bemused by a chill breeze that washed over him and he

was instantly filled with suspicion. He sat up quickly, fully awake and alert. Now he knew what had disturbed his sleep: the sound of the Kryptos door closing. He glanced again at Folly and this time he could see what he had missed before. She was not under the heaped-up blankets; the bed was empty.

What was she up to? All those warnings about the dangers of the salt marsh and here she was going off on her own in the middle of the night. At least he thought it was the middle of the night. He reached into his trouser pocket and took out a small Degringoladian timepiece, another ill-gotten gain. He had brought one of his own to the city, but soon enough he had wanted one that showed Antithican time. At first he had been a little confused with the Degringoladian method of measuring the passing hours, but not any more. In fairness, it was not a complicated system, just different. His new timepiece was marked like the Kronometer, divided into the four sections of the day: Nox, Lux, Prax and Crex, Nox being the longest. Vincent was right about the time, the hand was still in Nox, but Lux was approaching.

The Antithican year, he had discovered, also had its eccentricities, having thirteen months, not twelve. Citrine had explained to him how the thirteen pillars of the Kronometer represented those months. The Festival of the Lurids came at the end of the tenth month. Gevra, the coldest season, lasted

four months and the new year began in Torock, the season of growth. Now they were well into the eleventh month, with little to look forward to but more snow and Caligo, the thirteenth and coldest month of all. Vincent remembered how he had declared in his cavalier fashion that he could leave the city at any time. He knew that window of opportunity was fast closing. The barren plain would be snowbound by now. He would be mad to try to cross it.

Jonah was in a deep sleep, flat out on his back in the niche in the wall where Lady Degringolade's casket had been. His finger-knitted hands were resting on his chest and his loud snoring reverberating around the tomb

Quietly Vincent got up and pulled on his boots. He patted his pockets, checking his supply of black beans and Natron disperser (he had replenished them after the attack in the manor). Other pockets contained his father's picklocks, his knife, a coil of rope and a grapnel to replace the one he had left behind on his last escape (his encounter with Constable Weed seemed an age ago now!). He also had a Brinepurse, containing the special Natron crystals that repelled Superents. Usually the Degringoladians would have dispensed with their Brinepurses after the Ritual of Appeasement, but after all the hoo-ha at the Tar Pit they weren't taking any chances and most were still carrying them.

Vincent crept to the door and opened it, cringing at the

scraping sound (Jonah had managed to straighten it a little, but not enough to fully rectify the problem). He froze when Citrine suddenly sighed and shifted in her bed, but then she settled down again and he slipped out into the cold, snow-covered Komaterion.

At first Vincent saw no sign of Folly. He was about to use his smitelight when he spotted the yellow glow of her manuslantern up ahead, so, keeping a safe distance between them, he followed as quietly as he could. He was not yet at ease with the overgrown terrain (he was much more at home on the cobbled streets of urbanity) and was further hindered by the headstones and statues that had been damaged by the quake and now lay at angles across his path. He stumbled more than once and each time cursed inwardly at the noise he was making. But the bobbing light was still visible moving rapidly away from him. Folly hadn't heard him.

At the Komaterion gates Vincent halted and tried to ascertain where his enigmatic companion might be going. He could see that she had reached the fork in the path, one leg of which led to Degringolade. Her light took the other, towards the Tar Pit. 'Well, well,' he mused. 'Perhaps she does know more about Axel's Blivet than she lets on.'

He started on the same path but was almost immediately startled by a sudden flurry of flickering blue Puca lights. He had learned, through bitter experience, to ignore them.

Very soon after his arrival in Degringolade he had made the mistake one night of following them. They had led him down to the Tar Pit where, disorientated, he had nearly suffocated from the gases. He would have died if Folly had not come to his rescue.

Vincent was annoyed with himself when he realized that he had allowed the Puca lights to distract him again and that Folly's manuslantern was no longer visible. Without her to guide him, he was now in the dark. The moon was merely a smiling sliver at this stage in its cycle and the stars shed poor light on the treacherous marsh. He dug in his pocket for his own light, but before he knew what was happening something solid pushed hard against the flat of his back and he staggered forward on to his knees. An area of the soggy ground in front of him lit up and when he raised his head he recognized the cut of Folly's black leather coat and her heavy-soled boots.

'Hey!' he protested. 'No need for all that.'

'I thought it was you,' she said coolly. 'Why are you following me?' She held out a hand and helped him up. He brushed down his cloak, trying to think of an excuse, then thought, Why bother?

'I could ask you a few questions too. Where are you going? And why are you on your own? What about the Pluriba?'

'I have my Blivet,' she said simply. 'And that is why I

came alone. You don't have a good enough weapon. Or the experience.'

The last comment rankled but Vincent held his tongue. He was beginning to understand how to win Folly round and it wasn't with temper outbursts. 'Are you going to see Axel?'

Folly didn't answer.

'You told me that once a Lurid has been returned to its resting place it can't be summoned or embodied again. Was that a lie?'

Folly's expression was as impenetrable as ever. 'I told you what I thought was true at the time.'

'And now?'

'As usual in this game, things aren't as simple as I thought. It's all to do with the blood connection. Axel is my brother, which means there are some things I can make his Lurid do that others can't. But tonight I just want to invoke him, to talk to him. It might not come to anything. Are you sure you want to see him again?'

'Can he leave the pit?'

'No.'

'Then I'll come with you.'

'All right,' she agreed. 'I know it'll do nany good trying to stop you. But be prepared . . . for anything.'

Vincent couldn't tell whether or not she was pleased to have him along. 'You mean more Pluriba?'

'Who knows?'

Folly took off at a brisk pace and Vincent fell into step at her side. 'So you do have one.'

'One what?'

'A bone from Axel. You need one to summon him.'

'I'm not summoning him; I told you, I'm invoking him. There's a difference. And I don't need a bone for that, just a simple incantation and a few drops of my own blood.'

They had reached the edge of the Tar Pit now and Folly stopped and took a deep breath. One good thing had come of the fire: the poisonous gases had been burned off. For now the atmosphere was breathable, though hardly pleasant, without a gas mask.

Vincent, who hadn't been to the Tar Pit since the Ritual of Appeasement and the raging inferno that had taken hold of the lake and shore, whistled softly. 'Domne, what a mess!'

The ground was black with ash. The salt pillars stood like charred tree trunks. The tar itself was rapidly thickening with the change in the weather. It still bubbled and popped like a black porridge, but the oily skin that stretched across its surface was less giving. Here and there plumes of smoke swirled upward and drifted to join the mist over the lake. The ubiquitous Lurids, however, were as reliable as ever; out on the centre of the tar they huddled in a luminous mass droning monotonously.

'They don't come over these days,' said Folly. 'It's as if they are scared.'

Vincent found it hard to believe that these wailing Superents could be scared. 'Of us?'

Folly shook her head grimly. 'Not us, but someone, something.'

She stood with her feet firmly planted on the blackened shore.

'My brother the murderer,' she said to herself, still trying to believe it, to make sense of it. She sucked her tongue against the roof of her mouth as if trying to rid it of a sour taste, then, for the moment oblivious to Vincent's presence, prepared for the invocation.

She lit a small fire and scattered sesame seeds and a pinch of saffron on the flames. She jabbed at the tip of her finger with one of the sharp tines of the Blivet and allowed three drops of blood, almost black in the dim light, to drip on to the aromatic smoking herbs. When it was ready, she took a deep breath. It had taken her many nights to pluck up the courage to do this. She opened the Omnia Intum and flicked to a marked page headed 'Ad Lurides Invocandos'. Beside her Vincent shifted his feet, they were getting hot, and the sound reminded Folly that she was not alone. 'Perhaps you should stand back a little,' she suggested, and he retreated behind a pillar.

'*Luride, adeste mihi, soror sanguine, perfidelis, sponte, nunc.*'

The last of the words floated out over the Tar Pit and Folly and Vincent waited. The effect was swift. The vociferous Lurids increased their howling and became more agitated. One of the ghouls separated itself from the crowd and began to glide across the boiling surface towards the shore. When it was only a few feet away, Vincent shivered. Beads of sweat oozed out of his forehead and he was washed over by faint nausea. He didn't know if it was the smell or the mere propinquity of the Lurid, or both. He remembered vividly, despite his efforts to banish the memory, the feel of the Lurid's lips on his own when it had attempted to assume his body.

Folly was completely unaware of Vincent's discomfort. She was rigid at the lakeside, staring at the approaching figure. When it reached the very edge of the tar, she braced herself and looked it straight in the face.

It was no less horrific than the last time. The rotting flesh, the exposed skull, the sunken eyes. Domna, the smell! The appalling stink of decay and evil. The Lurid's recent foray back into the world of the living had done little to improve its appearance. Its face was as ravaged and repulsive as ever. It was almost opaque, but Folly knew that if she touched it, it would be cold, the sort of cold that burns like a white-hot poker.

But there was no doubt as to its identity. This repulsive creature was Axel. This was her brother.

CHAPTER 16

TEMPER! TEMPER!

'Axel, it's me.'

Folly was unsure how aware Axel in his present form was of his surroundings. The last time they had met he had been under the pernicious influence of Leopold Kamptulicon and his controlling ambergris pendant. She preferred not to remember what had happened after that, when Axel had taken over her body. It had been a vile, vile sensation.

Axel contorted his gaping mouth. 'Dear Folly,' he said, and his eerily pitched voice sounded almost amused. 'So you finally found the guts to call me to shore. I've seen you here, night after night. I did so wonder if you would dare.'

Folly remained unmoved. She knew when dealing with Lurids it was best not to rise to their bait. They were fickle, untrustworthy creatures, regardless of their earthly origins, with only one overwhelming desire: to be free. Axel continued in the same mocking vein. 'But where is the boy, Vincent? Surely you have both come to set me free again?' He asked the question with such

sincerity that Folly was caught quite off guard.

'I, er. . .'

Axel laughed, and Folly was reminded again that he now inhabited another realm. It was not a human laugh, but the laugh of a bitter shade condemned to a crepuscular existence, like a shadow in twilight, in the Supermundane realms. He snorted with derision and it was a horrible wet sound.

'Dear sister, I know why you are here. You have come to see what I know that could be useful to you.'

Folly nodded slowly. 'Yes, that is true. I want to ask what I was prevented from asking before. And other things. But also I came to see how . . . you are.'

'How I am? This is how I am.' Axel opened his mouth and breathed deliberately all over her, and she coughed and choked from the stink of the gut-wrenching miasma and took a step backwards.

'How do you think I am?' he hissed, all pretence of brotherly affection gone. 'Condemned for the rest of my existence to this pit of horror. Have you not seen the ghouls whose company I keep? Look at them. Hear how they shriek and wail.' Then his tone changed again. 'Ah, sister, my only friend in the world, I am sorry,' he wheedled. 'I did not mean to frighten you. What is it you wish to know? Haven't you read about it in the *Degringolade Daily*? I murdered an Urban Guardsman and I robbed a perfumer.'

'So it *was* you who stole the ambergris for Kamptulicon. I guessed as much.'

'Yes, but I was tricked by your friend, the oil seller.' Axel sounded indignant.

'Leopold Kamptulicon is not my friend.' Folly regarded her spectral brother with deep suspicion. 'And if you are so blameless, why then are you here? Only the guilty are condemned to spend eternity as a Lurid in the Tar Pit.'

Axel snarled, his temper as unpredictable as mercury. 'I tell you, Kamptulicon made me do it.'

'How?'

'He threatened all sorts if I didn't help him. He knew about you – I don't know how. I didn't want to do any of it, but he drugged me and tortured me and blinded me with this bright light, coming and going, coming and going. Then, when he had no more use for me, he gave me over to the DUG. I was hanged and found myself here, but he came back and used the ambergris I stole to control me.'

He seemed to calm down a little and began to whine again. 'Dear Folly, can you not bring yourself to find some ragamuffin on the street, some good-for-nothing little thief whose body I can assume? At least let me have a taste again of what it is like to be alive. There are strange things going on these days – I could help you.'

Folly could feel Axel's cold breath on her cheeks and the

smell of him was beginning to make her feel quite ill. He interpreted her silence as a refusal. 'I see then you haven't changed. Always thinking you're better than me, our father's favourite. Well, it ain't good to spurn your own. He taught you all the tricks – now it's time to do what is right.' He opened his mouth and screeched, '*Free me!*'

Behind him the host of Lurids took up the cry. '*Free meeee! Freeee meeee!*'

'No,' muttered Folly. 'I cannot. I must not.'

Without warning, Axel lurched forward and stretched out his arms to their full extent. His fingertips just managed to touch her on the face. Folly yelped at the burning sting and jumped backwards. Then, drawing her Natron disperser from her coat, she aimed it straight at the furious Lurid. Axel put his hands up, and it was disarming to see such a vile creature make a gesture of submission.

'No!' he cried.

Folly lowered her weapon. 'Where is your Blivet?'

Axel was now flitting about the shore's edge as if in a state of indecision. 'My Blivet? So that's what you want. And to kill me. Again.'

'I didn't kill you,' said Folly. 'You were already dead.' She repeated the question.

Axel came back to the edge of the lake, the limit of his world, and snarled, his face a mask of rage. 'And why should

I give it to you? If I even knew where it was.'

'I need it.'

A sly look came over the Lurid's face. 'Kamptulicon will help me if you don't. And then you will have no control over me.'

She remained expressionless. 'Kamptulicon? What do you know of his business?'

Axel danced away, teasingly, but he hadn't gone far before Folly barked out a word in Quodlatin and he came back, compelled by its utterance. Calmly she spoke. 'Very well, I agree. If you tell me where your Blivet is, I will do my best to find a way to free you. But not for long. You are a murderer after all.'

Axel released a long sigh. 'I'll tell you, but you won't like it. And how can I trust you to keep your promise?'

Folly brought her hand up to her heart. 'On our father's soul, I will keep my word.'

'Very well. Kamptulicon took my Blivet when he set me up for the murder.'

'So he has it?'

Axel darted about a bit before answering, sulkily, 'No, Leucer d'Avidus has it now; he keeps it in the Governor's Residence.'

'How do you know this?'

'Because I was there, after the torture, waiting for the Urgs to take me. Kamptulicon gave it to Leucer and I saw him put

it in the safe. Now, when will you do it, sister? When will you keep your promise?'

'Soon, brother,' said Folly softly. 'Soon. It's not easy, once you've been expelled from a body. I thought you would know—'

Axel made another grab at Folly and this time he was too quick for her. His hands encircled her neck and he began to haul her towards the tar's edge. With a roar Vincent rushed forward and hurled fistfuls of black beans at the Lurid and, with a wail, Axel released Folly and tried to rake up the beans even as they sank. Then he began to sob and wring his scabby hands before finally fleeing to join those whom he so despised.

Vincent helped Folly to her feet.

'Kew,' she managed to croak. 'He nearly had me!'

'We can get the Blivet now,' said Vincent excitedly. 'I can steal it from Leucer's safe.' He had a sudden vision of himself wielding the triple-tined platinum weapon. He imagined how it would feel to bliv a Pluribus next time he saw one. And if he got the chance maybe he would stick it in Kamptulicon too. What effect would it have on a human? Was Kamptulicon even human? He looked at his metal hand and wondered.

Folly just stared at him blankly, rubbing her neck where the imprint of Axel's hands had been burned into the skin. He realized that perhaps he was being too presumptuous. Maybe Axel was telling the truth and had been set up. Domne! What a place to spend eternity if you were innocent.

'I'm sorry. What Axel said – is he really innocent?'

Folly's laugh had an edge of sadness to it. 'So he fooled you, did he? I'll admit he is very plausible. But he is a Lurid, Vincent, and there's not a one in the Tar Pit would admit to its crime, whatever the evidence. I have little doubt my brother deserves to be in that Tar Pit, no matter how much he protests his innocence.'

'Oh,' said Vincent quietly. 'Surely then you did not mean it, that you would free him?'

'I made a promise,' she said, and Vincent thought he detected the hint of a tremor in Folly's normally cool tones. 'I don't break promises, but I *was* telling the truth. He has already assumed a body. That makes it a hundred times harder to release him again. But maybe Kamptulicon knows a way. He is a Cunningman; I am not. So much has changed I can't tell any more what is possible and what is not.'

With Lux fast approaching, the two made their way silently back to the Komaterion and the safety of the Kryptos. On the threshold Folly turned to Vincent and smiled briefly.

'So, my burglar friend, how do you propose to get the Blivet? The Governor's Residence is at the top of Collis Hill, reached only by the funicular railway. It's well guarded. You haven't broken in there yet.'

Vincent set his mouth in a firm line. 'Yet,' came the laconic reply.

Chapter 17

Paint Your Wagon

'Cockles!' exclaimed Jonah. 'What in Poseidon is that?'

Citrine, pedalating cautiously round the perimeter of Mercator Square on the way to the Caveat Emptorium, shot a fleeting glance at the thirteen pillars of the Kronometer and saw what Jonah meant. Each pillar was a-flutter and a-jingle with a multitude of tokens tied on by the superstitious residents of the city. There were all manner of offerings ranging from simple dolls fashioned from straw (the sort of thing a child might make) to silver pendants and bottles of rare oil and even coins punched and tied together like a necklace. And the value of the offerings also ranged from one end of the spectrum to the other; the donors knew that no one would dare to steal them for fear of dreadful Supermundane repercussions.

'Gifts to the Supermundane, to appease the entities. Everyone is upset. The business down at the Tar Pit was bad enough, then the earthquake and now the Kronometer stopping. This is the Degringoladian way of coping,' explained Citrine.

'I ain't never seen nanything like that before.'

Citrine resisted the urge to point out the multiple negatives in Jonah's declaration and concentrated on passing through the marketplace as quickly as possible. It was Prax, and she had thought that by now Mercator Square would be deserted, but in actuality it was quite alive with people and, more alarmingly, Urgs. They stood in groups, easily identified by their headgear, eyeing the passers-by and watching the traffic.

'You know,' said Jonah thoughtfully, trying to make himself as small as possible inside the vehicle. 'I'm not sure how long we can keep using this Trikuklos. The Urgs know we have one, and yours does stick out like a swordfish in a school of sardines.'

Citrine knew he was right. Generally people rode about on horseback or in carriages, and although Trikukloi were becoming more and more common, they were still an object of curiosity and attracted unwanted attention. And, given the fact that the other Trikukloi were single-seaters, Citrine's, being double and longer and wider, stood out even more.

Jonah continued. 'Vincent said that the Urgs have been ordered to stop and search all Trikuklos drivers, hoping to find us.'

Citrine pressed harder on the pedals, turned out of the square and shortly afterwards stopped down the dead-end alley beside Claude Caballoux's horsemeat shop. Together

she and Jonah hurried across the road and Citrine pushed open the door of the Caveat Emptorium to the tuneless accompaniment of the shop bell. When Jonah stepped inside, his huge bulk blocked almost completely the dull early-evening light.

'Would it surprise you to know,' Citrine whispered, 'I have never been in this shop?'

Jonah was not surprised. Wenceslas Wincheap's Caveat Emptorium, indeed any such establishment of barter, was not the typical haunt of a family such as the Capodels.

Citrine couldn't help but feel excited at this new experience. The last year in the Capodel Townhouse with Edgar had been very difficult. He had kept her on a short lead, isolated her from her friends and saddled her with a strict governess. She would never have thought that it would take a charge of murder to escape him. Of course, the prospect of the noose still hung over her head like the sword of Damocles, and she felt wretched about poor Florian, but there was no denying she was enjoying her new-found freedom, despite the complications that came with it.

'I've been here once or twice,' said Jonah. 'There's good fishing down near the lighthouse – but you must watch out for those gulls, vicious they are – and Wenceslas always has a supply of fish hooks and bait buckets.'

Their eyes had barely adjusted to the poor light when

a voice boomed out from somewhere further back in the shop. 'Well, well! I believes I could get meself a few hundred sequenturies if I turned youse in!'

The rotund figure of Wenceslas Wincheap manifested itself from the shadows and stepped into the light of his own manuslantern, which he helpfully held above his head. Citrine and Jonah stood aside as he squeezed past them and locked the door.

'Don't worry,' he said to Citrine, who had paled at the sound of the turning key. 'It ain't to keep you in, more to keep unwelcome visitors out. Now I can give you me full attention. Suma said I was to look out fer youse.'

He beckoned to them to follow him, and they did, down a short corridor and into a small back room. It was wonderfully warm and cosy and quite different from the dusty neglected shop. Wenceslas gestured to them both to sit down on the fireside chairs. The fire was stacked high with logs and was giving out powerful heat. The shopkeeper stood between them, staring from one to the other with his tiny eyes.

'I remembers you,' he said to Jonah. 'I still has that Cachelot tooth you etched, very skilful.' Jonah reddened; he was not proud of his whaling past.

'And I believes you to be Citrine Capodel.' Wenceslas shook out a rolled-up bill that had been propped against the fireplace. It was one of Chief Guardsman Fessup's 'At

Large and Dangerous' posters. It showed the four of them, the so-called 'Phenomenals', drawn in bold black ink, with the words 'Murderers' and 'Thieves' screaming out from above their heads. But it wasn't the words that were the most prominent aspect of the poster. Unusually for such 'wanted' bills, Fessup had instructed the printers to use colour, specifically for Citrine's russet hair. The facial likeness was certainly reasonable, but her hair was unmistakable.

Citrine managed a laugh and pushed back her hood to display a head of rather odd-looking hair, still a strange and tangled mixture of black and her natural red from the recent dyeing disaster. Wenceslas raised a wiry eyebrow, but said nothing.

'We don't want to cause you any trouble with Fessup or his Urgs,' said Citrine, 'but Suma said you might be able to help us.'

Wenceslas laughed. 'Urgs? Pah! Not a brain cell between them. I ain't worried 'bout Fessup's claptrapulation and his bungling pantaloons. Suma told me to help you anyhoos I can, and that's what I'll do.' He pushed his hand into his pocket and pulled out a small paper packet. 'For you.'

Citrine read the label. 'Hair dye?'

'Won't run in the rain, this one, Suma says.' Wenceslas went out into the shop and the two exchanged a quizzical glance as they listened to his rummaging about. He

returned carrying a large can.

'Now, you'll be needing something for that Trikuklos of yours – stands out like a sore thumb, it does. Your father always did like quality; only the biggest and best for Hubert.'

'You knew my father?'

'Oh yes. He came in all the time, looking for bits and pieces. You know what I say – sumthin' for ever'one in here. Now, I set aside a tin of this for you. Try it.'

'Paint?' queried Jonah.

'The Trikuklos is black already.' Citrine was rather taken aback at the revelation that her father was a customer of the Caveat Emptorium. 'How will this help?

'Not paint, varnish, and no ornerary varnish neither,' said Wenceslas. 'It dries to a special sheen that reflects what's around it.'

'Like a mirror?' Jonah sounded uncharacteristically sceptical.

'Sort of,' said Wenceslas. 'But it makes things much harder to see. It ain't perfect – it's no invisible paint, if that's what you're thinking – but on a dark night it does a good job of foxing any nosy Urgs.'

'Kew very much,' said Jonah, and graciously accepted the tin along with a couple of paintbrushes. Wenceslas, declaring dramatically that he had forgotten his manners, left to make a brew and soon returned with a tray carrying three

steaming mugs and a plate of hard cakes. Citrine and Jonah realized then how hungry they were. If they had been in the Kryptos, by now they would have been eating slumgullion. Citrine was also taking a little pleasure from the relatively soft furniture and the simple act of drinking tea. Folly's tisane was wonderful, but its flavour took a little getting used to. This tea reminded her of the good things about her old life. Wenceslas did not keep coffins and bones in his sitting room.

'So, how else can I help youse?' asked Wenceslas.

'Well, Mr Wincheap . . .' began Citrine.

'Wenceslas, please,' insisted the Caveat's owner.

'Well, Wenceslas, I wondered if you had some chemicals for my Klepteffigium so I can finish the Depictions.'

'Indeedy, I can certainly provide that,' said Wenceslas, and went and returned in a matter of moments with two blue, ridged-glass, cork-stoppered bottles, which he handed over.

'Anything else?'

I don't suppose you can shed any light on what Governor d'Avidus and Leopold Kamptulicon are up to?' asked Jonah, not sounding too hopeful.

Wenceslas sat and steepled his fingers and drummed out a little rhythm, the chubby tips undulating quickly, rather as a caterpillar moves. 'I know that Leucer d'Avidus, for all his pretence at being a man for the people, is a sly fellow not to be trusted. He has 'em fooled if they think he has their interests

at heart. But I ain't fooled. You don't have to go far back to see that the d'Avidus family are a bunch of troublemakers. Used to be in cahoots with Lord and Lady Degringolade, and we all know what an odd end they came to, a very odd end! Holed up in that big old manor, never seen or heard of again. I never thought I'd see the day a d'Avidus would be elected to run the city. I cannot say how he got elected, though it helps when you have the money he has. Money buys votes.'

'We know that Leopold Kamptulicon—'

'The "lamp seller",' scoffed Wenceslas.

'. . . and my cousin, Edgar, are colluding.'

'Colluding? Call it what it is, lass – hatching trouble. From what I know, it looks as if their plan, whatever it was, has been held up by all the ruckus at the Tar Pit.'

'I thought Kamptulicon just wanted a Lurid,' said Jonah, wiping crumbs from his mouth. He had devoured three cakes with gusto. Dipped in tea, they softened to a wonderful sweet mush.

Wenceslas looked thoughtful. 'Suma reckons that was a test, to see if it was even possible to embody a Lurid. Leucer has taken advantage of the fact that the citizens think your friend Folly is responsible for all the trouble at the pit. Ever'one saw that sulfrus smoke pouring out of her. All Leucer has to do to throw them off his scent is to keep up this witch hunt against you lot. It's no coincidence they've named

you the Phenomenals, after the worst Superents around. It's scared the people and stirred up their superstitious nature like a porridge spurtle. You've seen how ever'one still carries a Brinepurse even though the Ritual is past. And they wear their browpins and talismans and all sorts of whatnots.'

'We've seen the tokens on the Kronometer,' added Citrine.

'Strange things ahead, according to my cards. The quake really shook this city up. The lighthouse is on the verge of collapse. In my 'pinion, it's just another sign that something's afoot in the world of the Supermundane.'

'Did you suffer much damage?'

The big man shook his head. 'Oh, lost a few bits and bobs. It's the other stuff you should be worried about. The Kronometer and the prophecy. If you were a black-bean merchant right now, you'd make a fortune.' Wenceslas paused a moment, as if considering a change of career. 'If our governor can persuade the people that he is helping them through this dangerous time, then he has them in the palm of his hand for whatever he wants to do in the future.'

'Which is what?' asked Jonah.

Wenceslas shrugged. 'Whatever it is, it will help that he has Chief Constable Fessup and the DUG in his pocket.'

Citrine spoke up, unusually gloomily for her. 'I know what's in my future. I'm still wanted for Florian's murder. If I can't prove my innocence, I'm for the noose.'

Wenceslas made a clicking noise with his tongue. 'There's no denying you're between a rock and a hard place. Who do you think killed him?'

Citrine found herself unable to speak. 'We think it was Edgar,' said Jonah quietly.

'Family, eh – you can't choose 'em.'

Jonah got up and fastened his Cachelot-tooth toggles. 'We should away with ourselves. There's too many Urgs around for comfort, like circling sharks.'

Wenceslas led them back through the shop and Jonah marvelled at how the man kept track of all of his goods in the higgledy-piggledy mess. At the door, he nearly stepped on something and stooped to pick up a pair of odd-looking spectacles that were poking out from under a shelf.

'Aha!' said Wenceslas. 'So that's where they got to. Must have been the quake knocked 'em off. You have 'em. More use to you than to me. You can adjust the lenses using the screw at the side, to see near and far, like a ship's telescope. An old feller gave them to me. He told me all about them at the time – I'm sure he said sumthin' else too. Anyhoos, I put them on the shelf and forgot about them. And he gave me another thing. Now, what was it?'

'You wouldn't have a Blivet on board?' asked Jonah. 'My whale spear's no match for a Pluribus.'

Wenceslas started. 'Domne! You met one of those nasty

jelly beggars! That's not good, not good at all! I have to tell Suma.' Then he frowned. 'Did you say Blivet? Few and far between they are. Only Supermundane hunters and the like would have one of them weapons. I reckon a Blivet's more suited to your blonde friend.'

He opened the door and looked out, gestured to them that the coast was clear, waved and closed the door after them.

'I remember now,' he mumbled to himself as he shot the bolts. 'The other thing that old feller gave me, it was that metal arm.'

CHAPTER 18
KATATHERION

Rested from its exertions, the beast got to its feet again and began to walk. Tar dripped from its haunches and head and with every step it left behind black sticky footprints that showed six clawed toes projecting from broad pads. The Lurids had watched in muted fascination as the beast scaled easily the ridge up to the salt marsh and disappeared over the edge.

It went on, doggedly, snarling and snapping at the Puca lights which, though too quick to be caught, kept their distance. It ignored the path and travelled as the corvid flies. Even when it sank into the marsh it kept going, using its claws to get a hold in the mud and pull itself out. When the marsh became too deep, it swam, its paws like oars, propelled through the slime by its powerful thighs. It spat out the salty water and shook the mud from its scales. If it stumbled, it dragged itself upright again. Every few hundred yards it would stop and, its breath coming in a sinister rattle from the back of its throat, it would raise its giant head, black ears

erect and to attention, and listen, like a dog being called by its master.

Or mistress.

Finally it reached the dense forest that had engulfed Degringolade Manor. Undeterred it ploughed on, head down, forcing its way through the thick bushes and trees until it was out of sight and all that could be heard of its relentless progress was the cracking and snapping of branches as it continued on its way.

It approached the great doors of the manor and the multitude of trembling Pluriba. A few dared to challenge the beast and it ripped through their jelly bodies with its claws. After that the others moved away and let it pass.

Now the beast hurled itself at the doors, which broke under its powerful force. Once inside, it started to run, up the stairs and along the gallery, straight to the master bedroom. It stopped to sniff the air before proceeding to the dressing room. It rounded the screen and caught sight of itself in the mirror. It lashed out at its reflection and the glass shattered into a thousand glittering pieces. Heedless of the sharp shards all over the floor, the beast entered the Ergastirion and went straight to the chair where the lady sat.

'Katatherion,' crooned the mummy. 'I knew you would come.'

Chapter 19

Company

Vincent sat still and steady in his eyrie at the top of the Kronometer's thirteen pillars. For a brief moment he had turned away from his real target – the Governor's Residence – to look at the lighthouse. What the paper had said was true: it was at an acute angle now as a result of the earthquake. For the time being the powerful beam still shone out across the water at night, thanks to the innovative clockwork mechanism that kept the lens revolving, but if it wasn't repaired quickly the oil would run out and the lens would become so dirty that the light would not be seen.

He turned his attention back to the house on the misty peak of Collis Hill. Carefully he adjusted the screws at the side of Jonah's glasses, bringing the building nearer and nearer. He could see the wall and the gates and the two guards in the sentry boxes on either side of the gate pillars. The wall was about ten feet tall with a jagged top – from here it looked like broken glass jutting out from the bricks – clearly designed to wound. Governor d'Avidus made no secret of

the fact that unexpected visitors were not welcome.

He had often heard the clanking of the funicular railway, and now, with the glasses, he saw it quite clearly. It operated two small carriages, each just big enough to hold four people standing. The carriages acted as counterbalances for each other. They were both attached to the same steel cable and as one went up, the other went down. As he watched, the carriage at the top started to descend one side of the near-vertical parallel rails. He hadn't seen anyone get into it so he deduced that someone must be coming up in the partner carriage below. There were control rooms at the top and the bottom, each with a guard.

Tonight had been Vincent's first visit to Degringolade since that terrifying meeting with Axel. In the intervening days, the four of them had stayed within the confines of the Komaterion on account of the weather. They had kept busy; when not stirring slumgullion, Folly's head was buried in the Omnia Intum; Jonah sang shanties as he sharpened the points of his whale spear; Citrine practised her card-spreading and developed Depictions and, when she thought no one was looking, she looked at her locket, the one that never left her neck. Within it was her father's picture, but behind that was the broken fingernail she hoped would one day prove that Edgar had killed Florian. As for Vincent, he had taken the opportunity to hone his skills with the impedimentium and his metal hand.

He and Folly had told the other two about their strange encounter with her Lurid brother, and the supposed whereabouts of the second Blivet. In return, Citrine and Jonah had passed on the information they had garnered from Wenceslas and shown them the glasses. Citrine, always interested in anything novel, had delighted in them. Jonah had taken to wearing them around the Kryptos, claiming that they improved his vision, and Folly, predictably, had murmured that they could be useful. At first Vincent had laughed at the unusual spectacles, but when he realized that they could be used like a telescope he had to agree with Folly.

'Very useful indeed,' he murmured now as he folded them up, put them in his shirt pocket and climbed, as nimble as a monkey, back down the tower to the square.

It was already on the cusp of Nox as Vincent hurried to the Kryptos across the salt marsh. He didn't have the Trikuklos because when he had left on his reconnaissance earlier Citrine and Jonah were still varnishing it. Now that the marsh path had hardened enough to support the weight of the vehicle they had brought it all the way to the Komaterion rather than leave it at the broken arch.

Vincent drew his cloak about his face as protection from the cutting wind and sleet, and aimed his smitelight directly ahead. Its narrow beam zigzagged across the ground in front

of him, keeping time with his footsteps. Tucked into a pocket of his cloak was a copy of the *Degringolade Daily*. In other pockets were food and bottles of fresh lemon water and ginger ale.

Despite his outward confidence, he had to concede (again) that Folly was right; it was not going to be easy to break into Leucer's well-defended home, and not only because of the guards. Vincent understood his father's thinking, the importance of working alone, not relying on anyone else, but times were different then; the world made a little more sense. Now he had the others to think of. Yes, they were a liability – the last thing he wanted was to end up back in Kamptulicon's chair being interrogated about them and, worse still, possibly betraying them – but he had finally admitted to himself that he needed them, and wanted them, around.

There was something else though, something that Vincent was almost afraid to acknowledge to himself. Ever since the visit to Degringolade Manor and his encounter with the wrinkled mummy, he was filled with an unsettling unease that surged and ebbed within his veins. He couldn't shake off the feeling that someone was watching him. The lady's face came to him every night just before sleep and, when awake, he couldn't forget the sight and sound and smell of Axel. He hadn't realized how much it would affect him seeing the Lurid again after he had been in its burning clutches.

Vincent dug his numb hands deeper into his pockets, keen to reach the warmth of the Kryptos, and in doing so he discovered a hole in the lining. Something hard and cold had slipped through into a space between the layers of cloth, and his clumsy fingers took a few seconds to identify it. It was the compact he had taken from the dressing room in the manor.

He had forgotten all about it. He took it out and examined it again, running his fingers over the engraved surface of the lid. The pattern looked like some sort of maze, but when he traced his index finger along the lines he realized that he couldn't find a way out. He pressed the small button that released the lid and it rose slowly. Once again he noticed how the mirror seemed to give off its own light, so he could see his reflection without using his smitelight. But the glass was cloudy and his face was not clear. He rubbed it with his finger and his heart near stopped. *There was someone behind him.* He whirled round, his treen dagger at the ready, but there was no one there.

This place! he thought, snapping the compact shut and quickening his pace.

He almost missed the Trikuklos even though it was parked outside the Komaterion gates. Citrine and Jonah had finished varnishing and the result was quite astonishing. Even Jonah, who had been rather sceptical, had had to admit

that the strange muted sheen did indeed cloak the vehicle in a confusing darkness. Citrine had lamented the loss of the high-gloss finish that had made the Trikuklos so attractive, but equally marvelled at the effect.

Vincent wasted no more than a few seconds looking at the vehicle before hurrying on across the obstacle course that was now the cemetery. A movement a short way in front of him caused him to instinctively duck behind a headstone. He tapped off his smitelight. The slivery waxing moon came out from behind the clouds for a moment, but he didn't need its nominal light to see the apparition ahead of him. It cast its own eerie glow. He couldn't be sure what he was seeing. It wasn't a Pluribus, being pale rather than green. Could it be a Lurid? The apparition was motionless and, edging closer, he perceived that it was a person, a woman, dressed in a full skirt and a fur stole. The ladies of Degringolade wore narrower skirts these days. His heart quickened as she slowly turned her head and stared in his direction. He blinked and she was gone.

Maybe it was just a plain old ghost, thought Vincent, trying to reassure himself. 'The sort from ghost stories Father used to tell me. Lonely, harmless dead spirits that you would expect to find wandering about in a graveyard.'

In a place such as Degringolade Vincent logically considered that an 'ordinary' ghost would be the least malignant

of the Supermundane entities that haunted the region. More rattled than he wanted to admit, he hurried up to the Kryptos and slipped inside quietly. He smiled when he caught sight of the three-legged frog from the manor where he had balanced it over the door. Citrine had laughed, saying how it just proved he was more of a Degringoladian every day.

Folly acknowledged his presence with a nod. She was at the slumgullion pot as usual, wooden spoon in hand. Citrine offered regularly to take over but Folly always declined; there was something about the repetitive figure-of-eight stirring pattern that settled her mind and gave her a chance to think.

She paused briefly in her stirring to chide Jonah, who was pulling himself up through the hole in the floor. 'Hurry up,' she said. 'The slumgullion's been ready for ages. And it's cold enough in here without opening up that hole.'

Despite the recent improvement in his sleeping arrangements, Jonah had decided that he wanted to sleep in the large chamber along the tunnel. The Kryptos wasn't big enough for the four of them and he could sense that they were going to come to blows before too long. He lowered the slab into place and went over to the table, where Citrine was poring over a spread of cards.

'So, do they make sense yet?'

Citrine shook her head. 'Well . . . all things considered it

looks as if you are going to encounter danger in a low place and a high place. Maybe the low place is the tunnel.' She gasped and her hand went to her mouth. 'What if a Pluribus comes down the tunnel from the manor?'

'Pluriba only exist above ground, remember,' chipped in Folly. 'It says so in the Omnia Intum.'

Citrine looked doubtful, but cleared away the cards.

'Maybe it means Jonah is going to climb the Kronometer,' said Vincent as he came down the steps into the chamber.

Jonah laughed. 'There's more chance of a fish climbing up there than me.'

'You took longer than usual,' remarked Folly.

'I got waylaid.' Vincent wondered if he should say something about the apparition, but decided against it. In truth, the way he had been feeling recently, he wasn't sure that he hadn't imagined it.

'Well, I hope you've got something to go with this slumgullion. That *is* why you went out in the first place.'

Vincent grinned, took a facetious bow and produced, in the manner of a conjuror, a long loaf from one pocket, bottles from another, a bag of flour and some butter wrapped in waxed paper from a third. Folly broke into a smile as she accepted the haul. At the table, Vincent spread open the *Degringolade Daily*.

'Look at this,' he said, and began to read:

A Demonstration of Modern Science: The Power and Potential of Kekrimpari

All of Degringolade is in a fever of excitement at the arrival of Professor Arkwright Soanso, the most eminent physicist in Antithica and beyond, who is here at the invitation of Governor d'Avidus and Edgar Capodel. Professor Soanso discovered kekrimpari, a new and alternative energy source, which he believes will change the world. Tomorrow he will be staging a demonstration of his Kekrimpari Generator at the Degringolade Playhouse and all citizens are warmly invited to witness this exciting phenomenon. Entry is free, funded by Governor d'Avidus, and the show starts promptly at 8 Nox.

'My father was always talking about kekrimpari,' said Citrine excitedly. 'He said that if Professor Soanso ever came to Degringolade, he would take me to see his demonstration. Oh, I would love to go.'

'Maybe you can,' said Vincent. 'You can be sure practically the whole city will be there, *including Leucer*, which means the coast is clear for breaking into the Governor's Residence to get the Blivet. Domne, I can just imagine his face when he comes home to find it gone.'

Folly raised an eyebrow and returned to the pot. 'Are you sure you're ready for this? What do you know of the house?'

'I've been watching it with these.' He held up the glasses.

Jonah took them and his scars whitened under the strain of a frown. 'I wondered where they'd got to. I suppose I should have known; if there's a thief about the place . . .'

'Sorry,' said Vincent.

Jonah shrugged, not one to hold a grudge.

'Hmm,' murmured Folly, in that non-committal way of hers that infuriated Vincent.

He ignored her and continued enthusiastically. 'This is the chance I've been waiting for. If I am to stay in this city, I need a Blivet. It's not just the Urgs any more. There's something weird going on, and I don't mean all the shoulder-tapping and touchstone-rubbing and pavement-crack avoiding. Axel said it, and Wenceslas too.'

'And so did Suma,' reminded Citrine.

'And if we aren't properly armed we'll end up stuck in this Kryptos for good. We won't make it across the salt marsh alive. Black beans and Natron and stunners, they might work on Lurids, but they're no good against Pluriba. And who knows what else will come for us? What if next time it's not killer jelly but real Phenomenals? Everyone seems scared witless of them. How would we fight them off?'

'We won't have to fight off anything if you're not careful.

We'll all be in the Degringolade Penitentiary, waiting for the Carnifex to loop us with his noose,' replied Folly drily.

'If anyone can break into that place, I reckon Vincent can,' said Jonah quietly.

Vincent looked gratefully at the thoughtful sailor and suddenly the tension that had been growing was broken.

Folly held up her hands in a gesture of surrender. 'All right, all right. But I think you should take someone with you.'

'You mean yourself,' said Vincent. 'Look, I'm the one who burgles, you bliv the Superents. Let me do what I do best. I know what I'm looking for. I'll be quicker on my own.'

'I could be a lookout. And how do you know Leucer hasn't got a Lurid up there, hidden in a Cold Cabinet? He's done it before,' Folly protested. 'You haven't always worked alone. What about when you were with your father?'

Vincent blinked slowly. Folly had a point. What would his father have done? And to have a lookout made sense. Now it was his turn to yield.

'OK. It's a deal.'

'We need a plan then,' said Folly without missing a beat.

They all began to talk at once when suddenly Citrine hissed, 'Shh! What's that?'

A distinct scratching sound was coming from near the door.

'Mice?' whispered Citrine. 'Or rats?'

Vincent curled his lip at the thought, and the sound stopped.

'I hope there's not going to be another quake. The *Degringolade Daily* said that the animals were behaving strangely just before it.'

'I don't think it's a quake,' said Folly. 'Maybe it's time we made sure the Kryptos was a little more secure.'

Vincent thought again of the apparition. 'Do you think someone was out there?'

Folly shrugged, deadpan as usual. 'Now back to the plan.'

Chapter 20

Side Effects

Vincent was dreaming. And in his dream he was holding the compact in his hand and staring into the mirror. He could see his reflection, as before, but this time he allowed his eyes to relax and look into the distance, and gradually something else came into view. It struck him that the mirror was like a window and he could look through it to see what was on the other side. Now it was clear it was a room. A room he had seen before. It was the Ergastirion in Degringolade Manor.

By moving the mirror, Vincent found he was able to scan around the room. He saw again the shelves, laden with objects of thaumaturgy and, revolting as they were, he was compelled to keep looking. Fearfully, he noted the chair where he had seen the desiccated lady. She was still there, sitting upright, but she was no longer a brown, leathery hag. Now her face was fleshed out, and her dead eyes were shining, and Vincent could see that she was unbound. The straps lay on the floor at her feet, shredded.

'Vincent? Is that you?'

Vincent started at the silky voice. He moved the compact back up to the lady's face and stared straight into her eyes.

'Come here.' Her voice was smooth, so beguiling. She beckoned with her hand. 'You know the way.'

Vincent obeyed, naturally, as one would in a dream. He dropped down into the tunnel on to the crate that was now positioned beneath the hole and hurried away, straight through the crossroads chamber and on up the north passage until he came to the trapdoor. But how was he to get up through it without help?

There was something in his hand. He looked down and saw that he was carrying the crate. He didn't recall picking it up. He stood on it, opened the trapdoor and pulled himself up into the larder. Quickening his pace, with only the glowing compact to light the way, Vincent ran through the kitchen, up the servants' stairs and out into the main hall. The fallen curtains and the rotten carpet looked familiar, but now the corridor was marked with a trail of black footprints. He remembered the Pluriba and looked towards the door, only to see that it was hanging off its hinges. The jellified creatures were nowhere to be seen. He breathed in and licked his lips. He couldn't taste them on the air. His heart was bouncing around his chest like a rubber ball, but he knew he had to keep going.

Vincent took the stairs two at a time and followed the

footprints along the hall to the bedroom and trailed them all the way to the shattered mirror. Seven years' bad luck for someone, he thought.

He looked through the opening in the wall and saw that there was a light burning within. He could smell something nasty, like a damp animal, and a low growl emanated from the darkness. He hesitated and his fear threatened to overcome him. This was becoming one of those dreams that was almost too real.

'Hurry, Vincent,' came the voice again from the other side of the wall. 'I've been waiting for you.'

Vincent swallowed and stepped over the broken glass into the Ergastirion. The woman rose from the chair, and with the light behind her she was like a glowing silhouette. Beside her there was a dog. It rose to its feet with a horrible scraping sound on the floor and stood beside its mistress. Its head was almost as high as her shoulder. It had not hair or fur, but scales, and Vincent counted six clawed toes on each foot. Its eyes were red with narrow black slits in the centre.

'Spletivus!' he breathed, for he saw now that this was no dog but a hellish ugly beast panting and slobbering.

'Who are you?' he asked the woman. 'How do you know my name?'

'Vincent, I'm surprised! Surely you take the trouble to know from whom you steal?'

And he realized that he did know. That he had known all along. 'You're Lady Degringolade,' he said quietly.

'Yes. And you have something that belongs to me. Where are my cards?'

'I took them,' said Vincent, 'but I can return them.'

'You will, or you'll feel Katatherion's bite.' At the mention of its name, the creature beside her lunged forward and growled right in Vincent's face. He stepped back rapidly. He could feel its spittle on his cheeks. Thinking quickly, he held out the compact. 'Have this. I took it too.'

Lady Degringolade put up a pale hand. 'No. Keep it. Then you will know when to come.'

'Oh . . . and what about the cards? Shall I bring them here?'

'I will let you know.' Then, with a terrible swift grace, Lady Degringolade stepped forward and pushed him up against the wall and pinned him there with just one hand. Her face came down towards his and he saw nothing in her eyes but dark evilry. He reached frantically into his cloak and brought out a handful of beans. She laughed and struck his arm and the beans flew away.

'Black beans? Natron? I had thought my emancipator would be more intelligent than that. Someone who has escaped a Lurids' embrace twice. But you are a Vulgar.'

He stammered, 'Your e-emancipator?'

Lady Degringolade stared at him, her eyes full of disdain. 'You smeared me with your blood and broke the crystal ring and rolled the maerl, did you not?'

Vincent thought hard. Yes, he had bloodied her and rolled the maerl, but the crystal ring? What crystal ring?

Lady Degringolade didn't wait for him to answer.

'If you tell anyone of this, of my existence, I will kill you. But before I kill you I will strap you into this chair and I will haul before you any you hold dear and kill them one by one and feed them to Katatherion as you watch.'

Vincent nodded, rendered dumb with terror, and backed towards the opening in the wall. This was no dream. *This was a nightmare.*

'Say nothing of this. Go back to your friends and sleep.'

Vincent woke with a violent hypnopompic jerk. Sweat trickled down his forehead. He lay awake, eyes open, staring into the darkness, waiting for his heart to settle into a normal rhythm. He could hear in the others' breathing the steady rhythm of sleep.

'Domne, that was too real! I've got to cut down on the Antikamnial.'

There was something in his clenched fist. The compact. He slipped it back into the torn pocket. He rose and checked the hinged flagstone, satisfied himself that it was shut tightly,

and returned to bed with a tisane to help him sleep. His mind whirled as he sipped it, thinking of tomorrow night and the plan to get the Blivet, until finally, the mug drained, he felt the guiding hand of the Hypnagogue lead him to a mercifully dreamless slumber.

Chapter 21

A Demonstration of Modern Science

Mercator Square was alive once more with an animated throng of garrulous Degringoladians. But the atmosphere was very different to the Festival of the Lurids, when Citrine had been carted through the baying mob and had come so close to hanging by the neck. Then, as was traditional for the festival, the crowd had been dressed as vile Lurids and brandished weapons, and leered with blood-streaked mouths. Now they sported much brighter apparel, as befitted an evening at the theatre.

The Degringolade Playhouse was on the east side of Mercator Square. It was a tall building with a broad frontage and a rather magnificent copper dome, now under a layer of snow. Above the playhouse's newly polished double doors a huge banner proclaimed:

Tonight

For one night only

Professor Arkwright Soanso presents

'A Demonstration of Modern Science'

It seemed that the entire populace had decided to cast aside their troubles and had come out in anticipation of an evening of entertainment. The governor's offer of free entry was doubtless an incentive, as were the deliciously temptatious food stalls. The air was filled with the sweet smell of roasting chestnuts and baking potatoes and steaming horse pie and beer. The cold was no deterrent – Degringoladians knew what to expect from an Antithican Gevra. The ladies wore thick cloaks and furry ear-warmers and dug their hands into velvet muffs; the men sported heavy coats with broad mantels and close-fitting hats made from the fur of the Sylvan beluae. All were in a festive mood and the only evidence of the recent disquiet was the unusual abundance of glittering browpins and earrings, rings, pendants and talismans. Not forgetting, of course, the overt display of Brinepurses.

The Kronometer's token-adorned thirteen pillars jangled like wind chimes. The clock was still not working, despite the best efforts of the city's engineers and horologists, but there was no danger of the audience being late for the show. As 8 Nox neared, an announcement was made via a loudhailer,

encouraging the jocund crowd to take their seats.

From inside Suma's wagon, Vincent, Folly and Citrine watched closely. They had an excellent vantage point and could see quite clearly the entrance to the building. They had left the now near-invisible Trikuklos in the alley beside the horsemeat shop. Then, one by one, so as not to draw any attention to themselves, each had made his or her way to Suma's wagon and slipped in, unnoticed by the distracted crowd.

As was often the case, Suma had not been surprised at her visitors' arrival. She expressed great pleasure at meeting Folly at last, and welcomed Vincent heartily. 'And where is Jonah?' she asked.

A good question. Jonah, self-conscious at the best of times about his scars and his size, could not be persuaded to come out when the city was going to be so busy.

'I would be no more use to you than a rusty whale spear,' he had explained to Citrine. 'And if I come the chances are I'll be seen and you'll all be landed in the drink. Let me stay here. I'll fix up the crossroads chamber to my liking and keep the slumgullion warm. As they used to say in my business, "May your crooked hooks fall straight into the cod's mouth."'

'He thought he would be a hindrance,' said Citrine. She still felt guilty about the day she had dragged him into her troubles. He could never return to his job in the penitentiary

now. And, for all her promises, she had not yet paid him and he had saved her life!

'He's probably right,' said Suma. 'Now, how can I help you with your plan?'

'Well, while Vincent and Folly are at the Governor's Residence, I am going into the playhouse, to keep an eye on Leucer – and to see what this kekrimpari is all about, because my father said it was so very important. But for that I need a disguise.'

She then presented Suma with a basket of assorted bits and pieces all donated by Wenceslas Wincheap. Suma shook her head in wonder. 'I don't know where Wenceslas gets this stuff,' she muttered, and set to the task with gusto.

By the time Suma had finished, Citrine was barely recognizable to those who knew her, let alone to those whose only knowledge of her appearance was the image of the russet-haired, green-eyed girl on Fessup's 'wanted' posters. Although her hair was dyed black again, Suma was taking no chances and had tucked it all under a grey wig. She had caked Citrine's face in thick theatrical make-up by which she changed the shape of her jaw, and sculpted deep creases in her forehead and cheeks. Her eyebrows were now like two grey caterpillars crawling towards each other. With several drops of a herbal tincture, she caused the whites of her eyes to turn bloodshot and yellow in hue. Citrine blinked rapidly at the initial sharp sting, but after a few seconds the pain subsided and her eyelids merely felt a little scratchy. The colour of her irises remained the same, but overall they were now so rheumy and repulsive Suma said she doubted anyone would want to look at them for any length of time. But just to be sure, she handed her a pair of thick-lensed spectacles. The look was completed with a dirty cloak and ragged fingerless gloves.

'What do you think?' she asked the other two nervously.

Vincent nodded in admiration, and Folly, usually so hard to read, was obviously impressed. 'Suma's right – I doubt anyone will bother you for fear of what they might catch.'

'You'd better hurry before they close the doors,' prompted Suma.

'Keep your fingers crossed for me.'

'I can do better than that,' said Vincent. 'Have this.' He handed Citrine a small silver acorn. 'It's a good-luck charm.'

'Kew,' she said gratefully, and left.

'Wenceslas gave it to me,' said Vincent to Folly's raised eyebrow as together they watched Citrine from the wagon window. With her pronounced limp and hunched back she really did look like an old woman. Vincent would not have thought that Citrine, with her privileged background, would be so good at this. She had just entered the playhouse when a large Troika drew up in the street and two men stepped out.

'Well, that looks like Leucer and Edgar,' said Folly. Professor Soanso had arrived earlier to prepare.

'Now we know he's definitely in there,' said Vincent, 'we should go.'

'I'm surprised we haven't seen Kamptulicon yet.'

'That pantaloon'll be in there somewhere, don't you worry,' said Suma. 'Are you ready?'

Vincent and Folly exchanged glances, nodded and stepped out of the wagon. The ubiquitous corvid perched on the ridge of the roof watched them as they slipped away between the stalls.

At the edge of the square Folly grabbed Vincent's arm and held him back. 'Look who it is.'

A tall man was walking purposefully towards the playhouse and with each step his fluttering cloak flapped open to reveal the green lining.

'Domne, it's Kamptulicon,' whispered Vincent. 'Wait until he goes in.'

But he didn't go in, just strode on by.

'Why isn't he at the demonstration?'

'I don't know,' said Folly, 'but I think we should see where he's going.'

Skilfully they tailed Kamptulicon, matching his pace at a safe distance.

'Maybe he'll lead us to his new hideout,' suggested

Vincent, 'wherever that might be. I mean, he must have another Ergastirion by now.'

They slowed and watched as the Cunningman stopped outside the Caveat Emptorium, but he only glanced briefly in the window, and then hurried on to the horse rest-post at the end of the street. Shortly afterwards he came riding forth on a black mare, its hoofs ringing out their rhythmical tattoo on the cobble.

'We can't keep up on foot,' said Vincent.

Folly thought quickly. 'I'll take the Trikuklos and see where he goes. You go on to the Governor's Residence as planned. If I can, I will catch up and meet you at the funicular. If I'm not there in time, just go ahead without me.'

Vincent couldn't help flashing his trademark smile. 'So you do think I can do it on my own!'

'Never doubted it.' She winked.

Chapter 22

Let the Show Begin

Inside the playhouse it was standing room only. Edgar and Leucer sat in comfort in the box nearest the stage. Edgar leaned forward and watched Citrine elbow her way through the crowd to take up a position in the centre aisle at the top of the steps.

'Domne,' said Edgar. 'Even that old crone wants to know about kekrimpari.'

Leucer was busy acknowledging his admirers, regally waving his hand at the men below who doffed their hats at him and the ladies who nodded their heads towards him. Some called up their congratulations. 'A splendid idea, Governor, just what we need in these upsetting times.'

'Hear! Hear!' came a chorus of grateful voices.

Although Edgar would have preferred to spend his evening at the gaming table in the Bonchance Club, he could not deny that he was rather intrigued by this kekrimpari business. Uncle Hubert had mentioned it more than once before his 'unfortunate disappearance' (as Edgar liked to refer to it),

saying how it could be used for making chemicals in the manufactory. At the time Edgar hadn't paid much attention, but now that Leucer had taken an interest it behoved him to do so as well. In fact, Leucer had insisted that he come, and Edgar, being rather entangled with the esteemed governor, could not afford to upset him. Leucer d'Avidus knew just a little too much about the skeletons in Edgar Capodel's closet and, if he wished, could put him in a very difficult position.

To put it more bluntly, Edgar was scared of Leucer. He took comfort from the fact that as long as he provided the governor with what he wanted – money and free use of the Capodel Chemicals manufactory – he could enjoy the advantages of being closely associated with a man of such power and influence. Degringoladians admired their charismatic leader, and Edgar, always one for an easy life, enjoyed basking in Leucer's reflected glory.

He looked down smugly at the grateful audience. Overall, life was good. He had inherited all of his father's money, his house and the manufactory. He could do more or less what he pleased, and for the time being Leucer was happy to have him around. The fly in the ointment – or should that be flies – were Citrine and her new friends. But once they had the four of them locked up, everything would be just dandy. Leucer and Kamptulicon would raise the Lurids and he would have an uncomplaining workforce that didn't require rest

or remuneration. The Capodel Chemical Company would make a fortune!

Leucer nudged him out of his reverie. 'Witness, Edgar: if you give the people what they want, a little entertainment, in exchange they will give you free rein to do as you please.'

'Only because they don't know what you're up to.'

'Exactly. And what they don't know won't hurt them. I'm sure you agree.'

The two laughed and touched glasses and took a long draught of their Grainwine. Leucer was certainly in a very good mood. Edgar liked to think that it was partly to do with his plan to catch Citrine and her conspirators. It wasn't foolproof, but the chances were at least one of them would fall into the trap.

He felt a tap on the shoulder. 'They're ready for you, Mr Capodel.'

Edgar got up. 'Duty calls,' he said, and bid his companion adieu.

Citrine saw Edgar leave the box. She had watched him and the governor laughing and drinking and making merry, and the spectacle left a bitter taste in her mouth. It was odd knowing how once she had shared her life and her home with her heartless cousin. Blood is thicker than water, people said. Not in this case. She rubbed at her neck where the rough

gallows rope had burned her skin. It would be a long time before she could forgive him for that, if ever!

The lights went down, the audience hushed and the curtains swished back to reveal Edgar and another man standing side by side on the stage, lit by the spotlight. Behind them was a large irregular shape concealed under a black velvet cloth. There was a great cheer and the pair bowed and nodded and smiled and waved.

Edgar stepped forward and held up the flat of his hand. Eventually the clapping died away and he began to speak.

'Welcome, everyone, to the Degringolade Playhouse on this momentous occasion. No one will deny that the last few weeks have been difficult for both Degringolade city and her citizens. The Ritual of Appeasement ended in near disaster, and, shortly after, I buried my uncle, Hubert Capodel, such a great loss for me and the city.'

He paused to allow the murmur of sympathy to ripple across the crowd. The Degringoladians might be unsure of Edgar's integrity, but they too had mourned Hubert.

Citrine listened, anger mounting at her cousin's hypocrisy. She recalled only too well the empty casket in the Capodel Kryptos, the casket that Edgar claimed held the body of her father. His voice droned on.

'And we have just suffered an earthquake. I have been asked to take this opportunity to stress again that, shocking as it was

to us all, it was a natural phenomenon and its timing was merely coincidental. Although the lighthouse is still a place of peril, Governor d'Avidus wanted me to assure you all that the Kronometer will be working again very soon *(cheering)*. He also wishes you to know that every guardsman in the city is hunting down the vicious foursome dubbed so aptly by the *Degringolade Daily* 'The Phenomenals' *(booing and hissing)*. Indeed, they came very close only a few nights ago to capturing two of them. Rest assured, they will not remain at large for much longer. With Chief Guardsman Fessup's men at every city exit point, and with the expected Gevran temperatures, they will not survive for long! *(loud cheering)*'

Citrine, acutely aware that she was one of the Phenomenals, felt a little shiver of fear at these words and folded her arms tightly as if to make herself less conspicuous. Edgar was enjoying the attention.

'Now, on to the business of the night. I know that if my uncle was alive today he would have wanted very much to be here to witness this demonstration of modern science. So, without further ado, it gives me great pleasure to introduce Professor Arkwright Soanso and his amazing Kekrimpari Generator.'

Professor Soanso, a tall man with a large forehead and thick greying hair, came forward and took a deep bow to booming applause. Then, with a theatrical flourish, he stepped to one side and whipped away the black cloth . . .

Chapter 23

An Unwanted Visitor

Folly ducked quickly into the alley, clapping her hands to ensure any lurking city Superents were scared away. For a moment she panicked, thinking the Trikuklos was gone, but then her eyes adjusted to the gloom and she could just about make out its faint outline. Without hesitation she climbed into the vehicle and pedalated after the Cunningman.

Folly had not piloted the vehicle as many times as the others and got off to a slow start. As her confidence grew, however, she allowed herself to glance out to see her reflection in the shop windows. There was little to see; the Trikuklos was little more than a strange ghostly blur passing along the street. Wenceslas's varnish really was quite remarkable.

Soon they were on the unlit Great West Road out of Degringolade. Kamptulicon was still visible ahead, his manuslantern helpfully acting like a beacon. Folly didn't dare to use her pedalator-powered front lights in case he saw them. He was moving at a reasonable pace, but certainly not in a hurry. Presently the horse veered off the main road and went

through the derelict gates of Degringolade Manor, carefully negotiating the broken arch. Where was Kamptulicon going? Not to the manor itself, for man and mare turned and started on the icy path across the salt marsh, the path that led to the Komaterion.

Folly slowed and struggled somewhat to steer the Trikuklos over the hard ground. The going was tough, the road uneven, but the superior suspension – only available on this model – served its purpose well and, despite the ruts, the machine kept going noiselessly and with surprising comfort for the pilot.

A creeping feeling of doom came over her as Kamptulicon dismounted at the gates, tied his horse to the railings and entered the Komaterion. Leaving the Trikuklos out of sight she followed cautiously. He too appeared to be proceeding with some caution and Folly was rather perturbed at this. Did he suspect that he might meet someone here? Did he know about their hideout?

Hoping to get ahead of Kamptulicon and warn Jonah, Folly decided to skirt the outer edge of the Komaterion. But it was a mistake. She had not reckoned on the density of the tangled undergrowth and the low spreading branches, and she struggled to get through. Finally the Kryptos came into sight. The burial chamber looked abandoned and there was no evidence from the outside of their comings and goings – Folly had always been meticulous about covering their tracks – and the door was so well-sealed it did not allow any light to escape.

At least that was how it used to be.

Not any more. Folly's heart plummeted when she saw the smallest chink of light between the door and the frame. 'It must be since the earthquake,' she thought. 'Oh, why didn't I check!' And worse still, she didn't know if the light was on because Jonah was in there or Kamptulicon.

A deep rumble filled her ears and the earth beneath her feet began to shake. 'Not again!' She grabbed a branch to steady herself.

Kamptulicon had only recently considered the Kryptos as a possible Ergastirion. Then, when he had come that night to investigate it properly, he had seen the light from the door and knew that something was not as it should be. In his experience, the dead rarely needed the benefit of an oil lamp.

Tonight, unaware that Folly was behind him, he had reached the Kryptos vital minutes ahead of her. There was no sign of life, but still he took no chances and listened at the door for some moments. Then, using the skeleton key so helpfully provided (at great cost) by Will Van Clefhole, he had let himself in, his blinding spergo liquid at the ready in one hand and a drawn dagger in the other.

Having satisfied himself that the chamber was empty,

he had barely rasped a Fulger's Firestrike down the rough stone wall and lit a lamp before the earth had heaved and knocked him to the floor for the second time that week. He cursed loudly. Luckily the tremor proved to be a short, milder aftershock lasting only a matter of seconds, and when it was over he stood up, dusted himself off and took a proper look around.

Kamptulicon was quite delighted with what he saw. The building was eminently suited to his needs: it was out of the way, deceptively spacious, and the fireplace – a traditional feature in Kryptoi – was pleasingly large. There was a pot hanging over the glowing coals and he smelled the distinct aroma of stew. Of course, he would have to get rid of whoever was living here, a vagrant no doubt, but no one would miss such a person.

He sheathed his knife, pocketed the spergo and descended the steps. He noted Lady Degringolade's damaged coffin on the floor, a casualty of the earthquake, but apart from that he saw the unmistakable accoutrements of not the dead but the living: clothing, cutlery and crockery.

He picked up, examined and carefully replaced various objects. He looked at the empty wine bottles and was astonished at the labels. He noted the quality of the crockery and the gleam of the silverware and the thickness of the blankets so casually thrown across the bedrolls. 'Feather pillows?' This was the hideaway of a vagrant with refined tastes and a penchant for the finer things in life.

It was then he was struck as if by a bolt of Professor Soanso's kekrimpari.

'I'm in the lair of the Phenomenals!'

It was patently obvious now that all these things had been stolen by Vincent Verdigris. Kamptulicon felt a grudging admiration for the metal-handed thief, the bane of his life. He counted only three bedrolls, so one of them was living elsewhere, most likely the Capodel girl, the cousin of that fop Edgar. He could understand why a rich, sophisticated girl like that wouldn't want to rough it in a place like this. Perhaps an ally of hers was hiding her somewhere in the city. Whoever it was, they would swing for it. He took three short blonde hairs from one of the bedrolls, Folly's, and put them carefully on to a piece of newspaper and folded it twice to contain them, then he searched the chamber methodically but quickly, fully aware that Vincent and his gang could be back at any moment. He was hoping to find his Omnia Intum, though he suspected Folly probably carried it with her. Whatever these kids were, they weren't stupid. To have evaded the Urban Guardsmen for this long was proof of that. Kamptulicon wondered, and not for the first time, if they really did have the Supermundane on their side. But there was no evidence of that here. Maybe they had just been lucky.

Chapter 24

Less Haste, More Speed

Folly pressed down hard on the Trikuklos pedalators, desperate to get back to Degringolade as quickly as she could to warn Citrine and Vincent about Kamptulicon. They had agreed to meet at the Caveat Emptorium later that evening; Citrine was to go there after the kekrimpari demonstration. She and Vincent were to make their way there when they had stolen the Blivet. She felt uncomfortable about leaving Jonah, but time was against her, and the chances were he would be perfectly safe in the tunnel. At least as long as no other marauding Superents turned up. The problem now was that Kamptulicon had a head start. He could gallop across the salt marsh faster than she could pedalate. He was more than likely going for the Urgs, and the last thing she wanted was to meet him coming back.

She grunted with the effort of piloting the vehicle. The return journey was proving to be harder. Not only was it sleeting, but also the narrow path away from the Komaterion sloped upward, making it more difficult to get the machine

going. *Tsk*ing in frustration, she pushed harder on the pedalators, managing to get a little momentum, but the next minute the Trikuklos jerked violently, turned from the path, then travelled across the marsh for a second or two before keeling over to land on its side in the salty, slushy sludge.

Folly lay quite dazed in a heap inside the vehicle. The Trikuklos was flat on its side. Dizzy, she got to her feet and stood on the door that now served as the floor. She felt for and found her manuslantern, but could tell from the smell that it had spilt its tarry fuel. Using the steering handlebars as a step, she managed to push open the door above her and clamber out on to the side of the vehicle. A blast of icy air caused her to breathe in sharply. The sky was full of snow clouds, and it was impossible to see which way she was facing – towards the path or away out on to the treacherous marsh.

'Oh, spletivus!'

Somehow Vincent's favourite expletive seemed eminently suitable for the occasion. Wishing for a smitelight, she sniffed the air and listened intently for any sound that might guide her back to the path. She couldn't be that far away from it. The Trikuklos had only rolled a little before tipping over. She climbed back into the vehicle and flicked the switch for the front lights, hoping that they had enough power stored up in the energy cell from her furious pedalating to last until she got

back to the path. They came on, albeit weakly – affected no doubt by the cold – and with a silent thank-you to Citrine's father for buying the very best Trikuklos that was available, she lowered herself on to the icy but reasonably solid ground. She took a tentative step forward – the light was behind her so she was walking in her own shadow – then another and another.

The lights flickered inauspiciously and Folly was grateful to see that she was almost at the path. Elated she hastened and took three quick steps forward, but with the fourth step her foot landed heavily. What she had thought was solid ground gave way to slushy water and she found herself plunging into a deep wet hole of freezing slime. Helplessly she flailed her arms about, her thrashing feet seeking purchase in the thick mud, but she kept on sinking. And then the lights went out and the last thing she remembered thinking before her head went under was how the slime tasted salty.

Jonah sat alone in the underground chamber, engaged in ponderous thought. He wasn't sure how long it had been now since Folly had left, but it felt like an age. He considered his position. Was it really only a week or two ago that he had been happily – perhaps that was an exaggeration – working at the Degringolade Penitentiary, living a quiet life away from the public eye? How much had changed! Now he was sleeping underground, afraid to show his face for fear of being arrested and thrown into the very jail where he had so recently been employed. Was that, as Citrine might have said, irony?

'And I regret none of it,' he avowed to the emptiness. He had done what he had to do. He could not have left Citrine to such an unjust fate, facing death by hanging, betrayed by her own cousin whom she had treated as a brother.

That didn't change the fact that he was now in a quandary. It was worrying in the extreme to know that Kamptulicon had found their hideout. Folly had said to wait at the trapdoor in the northern tunnel. So, he supposed, he should do that. But she seemed to have been gone an awfully long time.

What about the other tunnels? The south led back to the Kryptos and that was blocked, but there was still east and west. He tried to envisage the landscape above him and concluded that Degringolade itself must be to the east. Surely it would not do any harm to look down that tunnel. He had his spear and a manuslantern and his courage. What more could he need?

Folly opened her eyes, but the blackness around her was so complete that she had to blink to make sure they really were open. Her head was aching and her mouth was dry. She licked her lips and tasted salt and remembered what had happened.

Was she dead? She had certainly thought she would drown

in the slime. She felt her leather coat. It was heavy with damp and caked in mud. Her feet and fingers were cold, but she was definitely alive. She breathed warm air on to her hands and rubbed them together. She couldn't put her finger on it, but she had the feeling that something was missing. Her hand went to her belt; her Blivet was gone.

'Hello!' she called out softly, sitting up. 'Is anyone there?'

Her echoing voice confirmed that she was under the shelter of a roof, in some sort of cave perhaps. She stood and made painful contact with a low ceiling.

'Ow!' She dropped to the floor again, rubbing her head. She began to crawl on all fours and reached a rocky wall. She made her way along it slowly, but she could not feel a door and for all she knew she was going round in circles so she sat against the wall again, wondering what to do.

It was then the whispering began, at first very soft, but quickly becoming louder and louder. Folly tried to quell the fear that was rising inside her. She was certain that she could hear footsteps too. But she could see nothing and, strain her ears as she might, she could not make out a word of what the voices were saying.

'Who are you?' she asked, her steady voice belying how she really felt. 'Show yourselves, please.'

The whispering stopped abruptly and a second later the darkness was lit up with a score of dancing blue lights, like candle flames. There came the sound of laughter, the lightest laughter she had ever heard, and behind the lights, for the very first time, she could see what she had always suspected was there: a host of delicate long-legged small-headed dancing figures.

'Oh my,' she breathed. 'You're the Puca.' And she started to laugh too.

Having tramped for some time along the eastern tunnel, Jonah was reaching the point where he had to decide whether to go on into the unknown, or to return and make his way to the manor as agreed. This tunnel showed no sign of going upward to the surface. It was long and straight and by the weak light of his manuslantern he couldn't see an end to it. He had no idea if he was any nearer to Degringolade, or if he was even going in the right direction.

Then, to his dismay, he came to a fork and this time there were no helpful markings to indicate direction. He stopped and stood with his hands on his hips.

'Looks like the decision has been made for me,' he said.

He adjusted the whale spear on his shoulder and was about to retreat when his hand brushed against a lump in his coat. Wenceslas's glasses. He had forgotten he had them.

'I wonder,' he mused, and put them on. They balanced quite well on the bridge of his nose, but the arms were tight

on the side of his head. They were not designed for a skull the size of his.

'Now, what was it Wenceslas said?' he murmured. 'Twist the screws and they act like a telescope.'

He felt for the screws at the sides of the lenses and began to turn them simultaneously, no easy task with his huge fingers. He went to one branch of the fork, placed the lantern on the ground in the entrance and stared straight ahead. With each twist he could see that the darkness beyond seemed a little brighter. He kept on turning the screws and was surprised when shapes began to appear in the darkness. Blurry, moving shapes.

'John Dory McCrory,' he muttered. 'Now what's this all about?'

He turned the screws another one hundred and eighty degrees. The edges of the shapes became more sharply defined. Now they had limbs, arms and legs and heads. They were still some distance away, but Jonah knew already that they weren't human. He could smell them. That ain't Lurid stink neither, he thought.

He was right. This wasn't the smell of decaying flesh, it was more like a lady's perfume, but it was in no way pleasant or alluring. It was nauseatingly sweet. Involuntarily he curled his lip and spat, trying to get the taste of it out of his mouth. He pulled up his collar and shielded his mouth and nose, but

the choking perfume permeated the thick wool.

Jonah began to back away as the figures advanced. He remembered the black beans in his pocket and threw a handful down the tunnel, peppering the ground at the creatures' feet. With a sinking heart he sensed that the beans had annoyed rather than deterred them. They were coming more quickly so he sprayed a long burst of Natron at them. Again, it had no effect other than to obviously infuriate them.

The riled creatures were now so close that Jonah could see into their open mouths. Rows and rows of needle-like teeth were set in red gums that dripped with sticky mucus. The atmosphere was heavy with an almost tangible malevolence that increased as they came closer and closer.

Jonah reached over his shoulder for his whale spear. Slowly, deliberately, he brought it round and raised his arm and prepared to throw. In his heart he knew that his trusted weapon would be of no use against these Superents, whatever they were. He almost wished they were Lurids or a Pluribus. At least then he would die knowing what had killed him. But to be felled by a nameless monster? It didn't seem right.

The freakish fiends were well within range now and Jonah realized that, for all their menace, they had made not a sound between them.

'Poseidon!' he cried, and hurled the spear into their midst. And then they were upon him.

Chapter 25

An Exchange

When the merriment died down, Folly leaned forward to see the Puca closer. They shied away and their flames dimmed, but she could feel that they were giving off heat. Makes a change, she thought. Most Superents were freezing.

'Can you help me?' she asked gently. She was wary and a little fearful. They were known, after all, for their deceitful guidance. 'How did I get here? Did you save me from the marsh?'

The flames brightened again and the oval-shaped heads nodded vigorously. One of the figures came closer and she perceived that it was wearing a short close-fitting tunic of some sort. It gesticulated with its slim pale arms and hands and spoke in a whispery voice, exactly the way, Folly realized, she had always imagined they would sound.

'We saved you,' it said. 'You're safe now.'

'But I have to get back to Degringolade,' said Folly quickly. 'To tell the others that Kamptulicon—'

At the mention of Kamptulicon's name all the Puca began to hiss and their flames became very bright, almost white.

'Leopold Kamptulicon is no friend of ours,' said the one that had spoken. It seemed to be in charge.

'Domna, nor mine,' said Folly hastily. 'I have to warn my friends. They are in danger from him.' Then she remembered. 'Do you have my Blivet? I will need it.'

There was silence and the blue lights dimmed almost to extinction. Another Puca stepped forward. 'We took your Blivet – it is a nasty weapon.'

'I would not use it on you!' declared Folly. 'But on Pluriba and Lurids and other Superents.'

'We have seen the Pluriba,' said the first Puca.

'I know,' said Folly. And you didn't help me then, she thought.

'And the beast,' said another, but Folly wasn't interested in beasts, only escape. She persisted. 'Please let me go,' she persisted.

'Let you go? Of course we will let you go.'

Folly sensed a certain hesitation in the Puca's voice. 'Then show me the way out. Am I in one of the tunnels under the marsh?'

'Yes. But what will you give us in exchange?' The Puca's tone had changed and Folly was reminded of how Axel had switched with such ease between playfulness and menace.

'Give you? What do you mean? Not my Blivet!'

'No.'

'Then what?'

The Puca came right up to her and began to whisper into her ear.

Folly walked quickly and carefully over the rocky ground, head slightly dipped on account of the low roof, her hand resting on her Blivet, drawing comfort from the familiar object. She was still shaken from her encounter with the Puca. She looked over her shoulder more than once, worried that they might be following her or, worse, had played a trick on her and had not shown her the way out but instead a way into danger. Wasn't that what they usually did, she asked herself, lead people into peril? Her fears were countered somewhat by the fact that they had at least given her a light, a knot of reeds soaked in some sort of liquid that was burning brightly. The 'chief' Puca said that it would last an hour or so, by which time she should be safe. And they had sworn solemnly to keep their side of the bargain, if she kept hers.

But she would think about that when the time came . . .

On and on she stumbled, damp and stinking of the marsh and feeling rather wretched. She wondered how Vincent had fared. Better, she hoped, than she had. He should be at the Caveat Emptorium by now, waiting with Citrine. And what of Jonah? She shook her head.

'Domna, let him be OK,' she muttered. 'Please.'

Chapter 26

Down to Business

Vincent stood, a shadow in a doorway, across the street from the entrance to the governor's funicular railway. The barred gate was closed and could only be opened from the other side. Just beyond it there was a control room and the moving shadow at the window suggested a lone guard within.

Vincent knew that he could not wait much longer. For whatever reason, Folly had not come. He hoped she was all right, but in the same way that she had expressed confidence in his talent for self-preservation, he too felt that she was well able to look after herself.

He was calm. It felt good to have real purpose again. All this sneaking about taking food and blankets, it was hardly challenging. And he was particularly pleased that his target was Leucer d'Avidus. If anyone deserved to be robbed, surely it was the Governor of Degringolade? He was practically asking for it. The circumstances were not ideal, to have to go up in the funicular carriage to reach the house, but when he looked at the other option, a sheer rock face now covered with

snow, he knew that even he, with all his climbing experience and grapnel, would not be able to make it. He took a deep breath. Time to put the plan into action.

It was a simple plan. The best often are.

Vincent crossed the road quickly and crouched down against the wall beside the gate. He unscrewed his hand, flicked the magnetic switch and set it down on the pavement. Then, using a large pebble of impedimentium, he started the hand moving, just as he had been practising. It moved slowly but without a sound and was barely visible. It crawled easily between the vertical bars of the gate and up to the control-room. There Vincent brought it to a halt and, using the impedimentium in a sequence of deft movements, caused the hand to 'knock' on the control-room door. Seconds later it opened, and the guard looked out and then down.

'Domne!' he exclaimed when he saw what was at his feet. 'What's this?' He picked up the hand. He turned it over and saw that something was gripped under one furled finger. It was a small corked apothecary's phial. There was a label curled round it and he read aloud: 'Sniff me.'

To Vincent's immense relief, the guard pulled the cork out and, as people are so often wont to do, blindly obeyed an instruction for no other reason than it was there. He sniffed tentatively and promptly collapsed just as Citrine had done when she had smelled Lady Degringolade's narkos potion.

After that Vincent worked quickly. He picked the gate lock with his treen picks, ran in, reattached the hand, collected the bottle and pressed the large red button that indicated to the guard at the top of the hill that someone was coming up. Then he pulled back the operating lever in the control room before running out to jump into the carriage as, with a loud clank, it began to climb the steep hill.

Vincent stood just inside the carriage door looking up to the platform above, where the other guard would be waiting. When he had travelled about halfway, at the darkest point, where the lights from below were as dim as the lights from above, he climbed on to the roof of the carriage. He lay flat and covered himself with his cloak. The metal was very cold and when it touched his skin he shivered. It reminded him rather too much of the Lurid's touch.

The carriage came to a halt abutting the platform at the top of the line. Vincent heard footsteps, the sound of the safety gate opening and a nervous and surprised voice: 'Governor d'Avidus, you're back early . . .'

There was a moment of silence broken by a snort of disgust. 'Domne! There's no one in there, again! I suppose that fool down below thinks this is funny, getting me out of me warm office on a night like this for no reason.'

He turned away and Vincent jumped down and shoved the fellow in the back so he stumbled. Then, before the guard

could regain his feet, Vincent sat on his chest and rammed the bottle of narkos under his nose. A second later the guard was out like a snuffed candle.

Vincent went straight to the exit gate. It was locked, but that was no obstacle, and within seconds he had it open. Cautiously he peered out into the fine mist. The ground sloped up then flattened out and he could see the Governor's Residence close by, no more than twenty yards from the terminus. He could just make out the guards at their posts by the gates. He had no intention of trying to get past them when all he had to do was scale the ten-foot wall. Besides, knocking out two guards was enough for the time being. No point in using up the narkos unless absolutely necessary.

Keeping low and enveloped in his cloak, Vincent went up the slope to take advantage of the cover of the tall pine trees that flanked the residence. He skirted the perimeter until he was well away from the guards and then lobbed the grapnel over the top and walked easily up the wall. He flung over the thick blanket he had taken to protect him from the jagged glass and climbed on to the wide top. There he surveyed the lie of the land. Even all the way up here, at the very peak of Collis Hill, he could still hear clearly the wailing of the Lurids. He wondered if you ever did get used to it.

Next he turned his attention to the large house in the grounds. It was certainly a striking property, in the metal

and stone style that was peculiar to Degringolade. The broad cobbled drive that led from the gates to the main entrance was lit by lanterns hooked to poles at regular intervals. There were lights on in some of the many windows, but no other sign of life. Vincent moved along the wall, keeping low until, when he was out of the lights' reach, he dropped down on to the lawn.

Vincent knew exactly how he was going to get in: from the roof. People didn't expect that, and he had spotted a way from the eyrie. The building was excessively ornate, providing hand and footholds in abundance. He gloved his metal hand to muffle any noise and scaled the west tower easily, pulling himself from gargoyle to stone corvid to grotesque and up on to a flying buttress that led directly to the roof.

Once on the roof he took out a metal bar with a curved end and began to lever up the lead from around a chimney. Then, as if merely opening a can of sardines, he turned the bar and effectively rolled open the roof.

Seconds later, he was in.

Vincent had done this many times before and crawled confidently along in the attic eaves, a thin wall being the only thing that separated him from the servants' quarters on the other side. Most probably they were unoccupied; it was too early in the evening for the servants to have retired. They would be either in the kitchens or, at least the more senior

staff, in the Degringolade Playhouse being entertained by Professor Soanso.

Vincent found his way almost instinctively to the landing. Taking stock for a moment, he pulled a piece of folded newspaper from his pocket and shone the smitelight on it. It was a short article from the *Degringolade Daily*. A small Depiction showed three men wheeling what looked like a metal safe towards the gate of the funicular railway. The article, by Hepatic Whitlock, read:

Governor d'Avidus Plays It Safe

A new safe was seen being delivered to the Governor's Residence via the funicular railway. Thought to be a Dual-Key Bertram QuadraLock, this is the very latest in safe design. Traditionally the Governor's Residence is home to many valuable artefacts belonging to the city. In the light of recent events, doubtless the governor is intent on thwarting thieves, especially Vincent Verdigris.'

Vincent had laughed when he had read the piece. It was almost a direct challenge to him, and he never could resist a challenge. 'What was it Leucer called me? A stone in his shoe. Well, I shall give him such a blister he won't walk until Torock or Gevra!'

Decisively he descended the stairs, resisting the urge on each level to explore the many rooms, trying to focus on the job in hand. He was certain the Blivet would be in the new safe, and chances were it was in the study.

From somewhere far away he could hear the sound of kitchen machinations, but the ground floor was deserted. He looked into the drawing room, and the smoking room, another drawing room, and a meeting room before creeping along a short corridor that he suspected led to the study.

He was right. Gently Vincent closed the door behind him and stood silently observing the room. It was no different to what he had expected: shelved walls packed with books, dark curtains drawn across the window, and a large desk upon which stood a pair of brass lamps, one at either front corner. The desk was tidy, with an inkwell, a large blotter and some neatly stacked papers. There were two fireplaces, one brushed and cleaned with an empty basket, the other a glowing dome of coals. A large deep chair was positioned to one side, mirroring another.

Vincent continued to sweep the light around the room, but there was no sign of a safe.

'I suppose that would have been just too easy,' he murmured. He remembered how in the Capodel Townhouse Edgar had concealed the safe as a drinks cabinet. Leucer could well have done something similar. But the safe he had

seen in the Depiction was larger than the Capodels'. He examined the walls carefully, counting the panels, looking for inconsistencies, knocking gently. But it all felt solid.

'Hmm,' he mused, thinking and looking hard. His eye fell on the second fireplace, in particular the polished back plate. It had a standard design in relief, a simple log fire, which Vincent thought odd. He would have thought someone like Leucer d'Avidus would have gone for something more ornate. There were three words across the top of the plate:

'*Decus et Tutanem*'

The same words as those on his browpin – obviously a common saying here. Now, what was it Folly had said: 'An ornament and a safeguard'. He rocked on his heels and kept staring at it. Then he laughed. Of course! Leucer had fitted the safe in the fireplace. He pulled out the plate and there it was.

The Dual-Key Bartram QuadraLock might have been the best in its class, but it was no match for Vincent Verdigris. The thick metal door swung open slowly and Vincent felt again the familiar thrill that ran through his very marrow every time he succeeded where he knew others would have failed. His mind was filled with a swiftly moving panorama of memories of his father. He saw again the look of intense

concentration on his face as he picked locks, the smile that meant success, he heard the laughter they had shared after chases and a hundred narrow escapes. And he was completely taken by surprise when he found himself suddenly wishing that Folly and Citrine and Jonah had been here to share this moment.

The moment of truth.

He knelt forward and shone the smitelight directly into the safe. What would he find? Money, most likely, perhaps some jewellery, documents that might be useful, *but would there be a Blivet*?

Yes.

Vincent reached in and grasped the gleaming triple-tined platinum weapon that lay on the middle shelf. It was pleasingly cold to the touch, a little heavier than he had expected and sent a tingle down his spine. He gripped it firmly and jabbed the air with it and allowed himself a little laugh.

'Hello, Vincent,' said a man's voice behind him. 'I believe you've been – how do you say it? – rumbled!'

Except he said 'rummled'.

Chapter 27
Kekrimpari

In the Degringolade Playhouse Citrine, along with the hundreds-strong audience, was utterly engrossed in Professor Soanso's kekrimpari demonstration. It was proving to be, as Edgar had promised in his introduction, an evening of delight, awe and consternation. As the professor's machine whirred and spun and sparked and crackled, in tandem did the audience gasp and cry out and clap and laugh.

Citrine knew her father would have loved to have seen something like this. In fact, it was so delightfully enthralling that she had to keep reminding herself she was actually there to watch out for Leucer and Edgar. When she did glance up at their box she could just make out the blurred figures of the loathsome pair – Edgar had rejoined Leucer – her spectacles really were very thick. Luckily they appeared equally fascinated with the display and were both leaning forward with their elbows on the balustrade to get a closer look.

Professor Soanso had begun with a simple demonstration of the Kekrimpari Generator. It was a most peculiar machine,

an intriguing incorporation of levers and switches and glass cylinders and shining metal and looping wires. After a few basic tricks – showers of sparks and brilliant lightning bolts – the professor had called for volunteers. One man came up onstage and pulled a handle that caused his hair to stand on end, prompting the raucous laughter of the audience. Another fellow had allowed the professor to attach clips to his thumbs and then he jerked about as if in a fit. He declared afterwards that he was in no way hurt, but felt invigorated and thrilled to his marrow!

'Ah, yes,' Professor Soanso had explained, 'kekrimpari is not only a source of energy, but also a potential cure for the many afflictions of modern life. Imagine how it could alleviate lethargy and sadness and mental distress.'

Then he had shown them yet another use: a candle-shaped object with what he called a 'kekrimpari wick' enclosed in a sealed jar. 'See,' he said, 'when the candle is shot through with kekrimpari, the wick lights up but does not burn away.' Indeed, the wick gave off a steady pale yellow glow. 'Imagine how this light could illuminate your homes and places of work. It is clean, it does not smell . . .'

Professor Soanso's enthusiasm was contagious and as the evening wore on the air of excitement in the playhouse was at feverish pitch. The show reached its peak with a particularly spectacular display of purple light arcing across the stage,

causing the hair of everyone there to stand on end. Citrine joined in the thunderous applause.

Then Professor Soanso, having whipped the audience into a near frenzy, radically changed the mood. He turned down the lights, the orchestra in the pit began to play a sombre tune, almost funereal, and he spoke quietly. 'Now, my friends, it is time to be serious. I have saved one final powerful illustration for the end. Do not be surprised if you leave tonight having forgotten all you have seen until now and remember only what comes next.'

He beckoned towards the side of the stage and his assistant came on wheeling a trolley covered by a white cloth. He positioned it beside the Kekrimpari Generator. The professor removed the cloth respectfully and, to an accompanying gasp from the crowd, revealed a body laid out on the trolley. It was a man, fully clothed in black tie and coat-tails and white gloves. But there was something odd about the face and it took Citrine a few moments to realize that it was masked. Her own mouth gaped as the reality of what she was about to see dawned on her. Quickly she looked up at the box and was doubly shocked to see that neither Edgar nor Leucer was there. She admonished herself for not keeping a better eye on them and half rose, but then Professor Soanso spoke.

'Mr Capodel, if you please.'

Citrine hesitated. She felt the all-too-familiar fear rising as

she watched Edgar stride across the stage to join the professor in the spotlight. Perhaps Leucer was with him, waiting in the wings. She couldn't be sure though, and she started to plan her exit.

'Before we proceed,' said Edgar, with a degree of sincerity that immediately made Citrine deeply suspicious, 'let me assure you all that my dear uncle Hubert would not have objected to being a part of this. In life he stated to me and to Dr Chilebreth Ruislip that he viewed his body as a temporary vessel for his spirit – and what a spirit it was! He told me more than once that if his empty vessel could be put to good use after his death, then so be it. He stated further in his will, for all to see, that his greatest wish was to advance science.'

The audience, not quite sure what to make of Edgar's assurance, began to whisper among themselves. Citrine, torn between staying and going, knew that something very bad was about to pass. Edgar continued.

'If there are any among you of weak and feeble disposition, with heart murmurs or raised bloods, then I urge you to leave now. I have given permission to Professor Soanso to do as he scientifically pleases with my uncle's body, because I believe we are about to witness a miracle.'

Uncle's body? 'Domna,' breathed Citrine. 'What in Aether has Edgar done?'

'Dear citizens,' said the professor, 'please, I beg of you,

stay calm. This is a great moment in science. You are about to be party to something that nanyone else has seen in this province, nay this hemisphere! Here before you is the body of Hubert Capodel, taken from his resting place in the Capodel Kryptos. You will see, for your own comfort, that the face has been covered. Mr Capodel was found in the Tar Pit and his appearance had been greatly altered.'

Citrine could not believe what she was hearing. Doubt struck her like a blow. Was she wrong about her father? Was this why the Capodel Kryptos was empty, *because Edgar had removed his body for the professor*? She took off her glasses and craned her neck to see if it really was her father, but from up here and with the mask, how could she possibly tell? But she knew it wasn't beyond the bounds of Edgar's cruelty.

While Citrine's mind filled with horror, Professor Soanso calmly attached a number of discs connected to long copper wires to the body's head. Then he pressed a button, flicked a switch and pulled hard on a lever. A belt began to spin and a humming noise started up, growing louder and louder. Suddenly there was a tremendous crackling, arcs of blue light played about the masked head, and the body, up until then stiff and still, actually moved. The arms rose, the legs jiggled and the head turned and appeared to try to lift. A terrible wail seemed to come from the invigorated corpse and there was a sickening smell of burning.

'No!' shouted Citrine before she could help herself. 'No, what are you doing? Have you no respect?'

All at once she could feel a thousand eyes on her and she realized what she had done. Edgar ran to the edge of the stage. 'It's the old lady,' he shouted. 'The old lady there!'

The spotlight picked Citrine out and she was momentarily blinded by its light. Then, seeing the Urgs coming for her, she sprang into action and began to clamber over the seats and the audience, who were greatly surprised at her agility, and elbowed her way through the standing crowd, racing up the stairs to the foyer. She ran to the double doors and shoved them open to the shock of the attendants, who had not seen an old lady move so fast before. Finally on the street, she stood for a moment looking all around. Where should she go? A corvid squawked above her head. *Suma, I'll go to Suma.*

She took off across the square, skidded round a stall and ran straight into the arms of a pair of waiting Urgs.

'Let me go!' she shouted, and struggled so much that her wig fell off.

Someone handed it to her and a heartbreakingly familiar voice said, 'Hello, cousin. Did you enjoy the show?'

CHAPTER 28

MORE SUBTERRANEAN PEREGRINATIONS . . .

Folly started. Was that a shout she'd heard? She took out her Blivet, held it aloft in readiness and hastened on along the tunnel. She could definitely hear something now, terrible sounds, yelling and moaning. She slowed at a corner and flattened herself against the wall. The air was filled with a sickly sweet smell, like a heavy perfume. Cautiously she moved forward to look round the bend. The sight that met her eyes would have been comical were it not for the very obvious distress of the person making all the noise.

'Jonah?' she said in disbelief. But there was no mistaking it: Jonah Scrimshander, the erstwhile Brute, was thrashing about on the ground, apparently fighting off and at the mercy of an invisible enemy. At the sound of her voice the stricken mariner looked up imploringly and Folly was shocked to see that his face and hands were covered in blood. His eyes were wild with fear and he was grunting from the effort of his own defence.

'Bliv them, Folly,' he cried. 'Bliv them!'

Folly rushed forward. 'Bliv what? There's nanyone there.'

'The glasses,' he gasped, jerking his head weakly in the direction of where they lay just out of his reach. 'Use the glasses.' And then his eyes closed and his head fell against the rocky ground.

Folly grabbed the glasses from where they had fallen. She put them on and immediately saw that he was surrounded by creatures of the most vile appearance and intent, possibly the worst she had ever encountered in her life as a Supermundane hunter. She knew what they were straight away, from the teeth and the smell, from the clawed hands and the sinewy bodies.

'Noctivagrantes!' she said incredulously. 'Sweet Domna, save us.'

But then she saw something else, barely more than an outline, just beyond the affray, on the fringe of the shadows: a woman, watching the battle. Her mouth was slightly open, her lips glistened and her eyes shone with cruel delight. Beside her, straining at a thick leash, was a great snarling beast.

Folly's only thought was for Jonah. She launched herself into the melee, blivving indiscriminately with one hand and thrusting the blazing torch into the throng with the other. It seemed the only way to go about the attack, there were so many. And all the time she could feel the woman's eyes upon her and hear the growling of the beast.

As each Noctivagrant felt the piercing tines of the Blivet, it jerked violently and shuddered before turning on its attacker. The wounded Superents opened their fang-filled mouths in silent snarls of rage, but before they could inflict their bite on her, they disintegrated before her bespectacled eyes. Others, seeing the shining Blivet, now dripping with their companions' ghouze, fled down the tunnel and disappeared into the darkness.

Panting, legs akimbo, Blivet poised, Folly stood, preparing herself now for the beast's attack, anticipating the pain of its fangs tearing her skin, puncturing her limbs. For surely that was its intention?

But the woman and the beast were gone.

A groan alerted her to Jonah's revival and she hurried to help him into a sitting position against the tunnel wall. He seemed a little dazed, but after a sniff of sal volatile he revived somewhat. Folly dabbed at his lesser wounds and wrapped the deeper ones in bandages from her satchel.

'Where did you come from?' he asked. 'This is the east tunnel.'

'Is it? To be honest I wasn't sure where I was at all. Let's get back to the crossroads chamber. We'll be safer there.'

Together, Jonah half-supported by Folly, they made their way fearfully back to safety. Folly looked over her shoulder

at short intervals, all the time expecting another unforeseen attack. Once in the chamber, both feeling great relief, Folly tended properly to Jonah's wounds and dosed him with Antikamnial.

'I think if it wasn't for these glasses you might well be dead,' she said, cleaning a deep cut on his arm. 'It would seem that the lenses, whatever they are made of, can detect otherwise invisible Superents. We have a lot to thank Wenceslas Wincheap for. Pluriba, Noctivagrantes – what else is coming for us?'

'And mainly since we went to Degringolade Manor,' observed Jonah, his strength returning.

Folly paused in her administrations. 'Did you see that woman?'

Jonah looked puzzled. 'Woman? I only saw those things and their teeth!'

'I must have imagined it,' said Folly with a shake of her head. 'Weren't you going to wait for me in the tunnel?'

'You took so long, I thought perhaps I could find another way out. And what about you?'

'Oh, I'll tell you later. It's a long story. Do you think you can keep going?'

Jonah detected a rare note of weariness in her voice, as if she was heavily burdened. He nodded and stood up. 'Through the woods?'

'No, I know another way, safer and quicker.'

Jonah managed a smile. 'You're full of surprises.'

'I find it makes life more interesting,' she replied, and set off down the west tunnel.

They had been going for a good half-hour when Jonah asked, 'Are you sure this is the right way? I mean, isn't this going away from Degringolade?'

'I have it on good authority that it curves back on itself,' said Folly, who was ahead of Jonah by virtue of the limited space.

Jonah sighed and they tramped on. 'Shouldn't we be somewhere by now?' he began just as they turned a corner and came again to a solid wall. This time there was no sign of a trapdoor anywhere.

'Aw, fish-guts, we're stuck.'

'They were telling the truth!' exclaimed Folly. 'I will admit I was beginning to think we were on a wild-goose chase.'

'They? Who's they?' asked Jonah, tetchy from his wounds.

But Folly wasn't listening. Muttering to herself, she proceeded to explore the surface of the rock with her fingertips, starting at the bottom and working her way methodically all over. About halfway up she stopped and smiled, pushed firmly and, to Jonah's accompanying snort of disbelief, the rock slid smoothly inwards and across.

'How in the seven seas did you know about that?' he asked.

Folly tapped her nose. 'Come on,' she urged. 'Let's get out of here.

They went through the gap and the stone slid back into place leaving no trace of its purpose. Now the passage had become so small they had to crawl. It sloped steeply upward and Jonah was surprised and greatly relieved when he felt a cold breeze and smelled the familiar smell of tar. Together they crawled up to the surface and emerged on to a rocky terrain. Spray and spume blew into their faces.

'Domne,' declared Jonah, smiling and licking his lips, 'I love the taste of the sea.'

For they stood now the two of them on the shore of the Flumen where its dark waters met the briny Turbid Sea. And opposite, on a small island, the lighthouse leaned alarmingly into the wind.

CHAPTER 29

THE STRAW THAT BROKE THE CAMEL'S BACK

Vincent was groggy. His head felt as if it was full of the thick wet mud on the banks of the Flumen. He was intensely cold, right down to the bone, and a breeze was whirling around his head and numbing his ears. Every so often a bright light flashed and hurt his eyes and then it was gone and the darkness returned.

He lay quietly – he was curled up on his side – in the gloom for a short while before trying to sit up, but the world swayed violently so he stopped moving. His hands were tied and his feet were bound. He sighed heavily. This was not a feeling unknown to him.

He was perplexed by the intermittent light, but perceived in its fleeting illumination that he was in a small metal cage suspended by a chain. Every time he moved the cage lurched sickeningly and there was the sound of clanking links.

'Spletivus,' he muttered, 'this is far from good.'

He peered out between the bars and strained to see around the space in which he was incarcerated. The chain was looped

over what looked like a broad beam and he was hanging in a room with curved stone walls. A staircase round one side led up to the floor above. There were three glassless windows in the wall, which explained why it was so cold, and when the flashing light faded it was still dark but there was a subtle tinge to the darkness that made him think Lux was approaching.

Vincent stared at the ceiling and was not encouraged by the huge crack that ran diagonally across it. Doubtless caused by the earthquake. There was a strong smell of tar and burning. He listened for footsteps, but all he could hear was a constant clicking noise above him. He frowned. This was a puzzle indeed.

How long had he been here? He thought hard and willed himself to remember. The last thing he recalled was the sight of Leucer d'Avidus standing behind him in the study. Wait! The Blivet. Where was it?

Vincent groaned and would have put his head in his hands if he had been able. It was all coming back now, fast and furious and frustratingly brief. Now he knew why his head hurt, from the blow Leucer had dealt him after wrenching the Blivet from his hand. And the narkos. He could still smell it faintly on his nostrils. Felled by his own weapon! And that was it. He had passed out and now he was here, wherever that was, waiting presumably for Leucer or Kamptulicon. But surely this place was not the Governor's Residence?

Carefully, more slowly this time, he began to sit up. This caused more swaying, but eventually he managed to lean his back against the bars with his legs drawn up in front of him. His feet were pushing against a dark mass. He gave it a tentative shove. It groaned and moved.

There was someone else in the cage with him.

'Hey!' hissed Vincent. 'Who are you?'

'I could ask you the same question,' came the groggy reply.

'Citrine!' exclaimed Vincent in amazement. 'What in Aether are you doing here?' Indeed, the dark mass was Citrine. The cage swung jerkily as she manoeuvred herself into a sitting position opposite him. There was barely enough room for the two of them. When the light flashed again, Vincent whistled softly.

'You're a sight,' he said bluntly. 'You look like a Lurid.'

He wasn't wrong. Citrine's thick make-up was peeling from her face and dried blood stained her collar. She yawned. 'Where are we? And Leucer and Edgar! Where are they?'

'I don't know.'

'Domna! I'm tied up.'

'Me too. Hold out your hands.' Vincent reached across, careful not to upset the cage too much, and began to untie Citrine's hands. She untied his and then they untied their legs, all the time talking.

'The Blivet! Did you get it?'

'Yes, but Leucer caught me.' Vincent heard Citrine make a strange noise, as if a sob had caught in her throat. 'What is it?'

'I've just remembered – at the playhouse, Edgar had a body. He said it was my father.' In a strained voice she recounted the horror of the night. 'The Urgs took me and Edgar drugged me, again.'

'It's becoming a habit,' said Vincent drily, and in turn explained as fully as he could how he had ended up in the cage.

'Leucer left before the end of the show. He must have known you were going up to the house.'

'It's my own fault,' began Vincent, but Citrine interrupted.

'Why!' she declared. 'I think I know where we are. We're in the lighthouse. That's why the room is round.'

'And that explains the light and the clicking. But what a strange place to leave us.'

Moments later they were both unbound, but still swinging in the trap. Outside the sky had taken on the very beginning of a glow.

'I think the sun is coming up,' said Citrine, and the atmosphere lightened at the thought. 'At least we will be able to see properly.'

At that moment there was a huge groan and the building seemed to lurch sideways. Citrine clung to the bars until the lighthouse settled again, albeit at a more acute angle. She

looked anxiously at Vincent. 'The whole tower is about to collapse. We've got to move fast.'

'I know, I know,' he muttered. He was examining the cage and chain, looking for some clue to how they might escape their pendulous prison. His cloak pockets had been rifled and nothing of any use had been left behind. He still had his metal hand though. It was gloved and he wondered if perhaps that was why it hadn't been taken.

'No point panicking. Let's just stay calm and work out what we can do. Now, as far as I can see, we're hanging from a beam that is attached, in the shape of a cross, to another beam.'

'Hmm,' murmured Citrine. 'I'm not so sure it's attached. I think it's balanced. Look.'

Vincent looked where she was pointing and saw exactly what she meant. Sitting on top of the other end of the beam from which their cage was hanging was a large wooden barrel.

'That barrel must be full of something, something heavy enough balance our weight,' said Vincent. 'It's as if we're a set of weighing scales.'

A sudden scrabbling noise caught his attention.

'It's only a gull,' said Citrine.

The gull, one of the flocks of large speckled birds that lived around the lighthouse, stood at the window. It eyed the incarcerated pair for some moments before flying up

and standing on the beam right beside the barrel. Then it flapped up and landed in the barrel itself, its body and head still visible.

Vincent and Citrine watched the gull peck into the barrel and then lift its head and swallow something. Another gull flew in, screeching harshly, and joined the first bird. It too pecked and swallowed.

'It's fish,' said Citrine in confusion. 'The barrel is full of fish.'

'Just what sort of trap is this?' said Vincent.

Now a score of gulls wheeled and cried outside the window and others were jostling on the ledge. Inside the barrel ten quarrelled noisily over the unexpected banquet. Five flew off at once, each holding their glistening prize. At the same time the chain began to slide jerkily down the beam as it started to upend, and the cage dropped slowly, albeit ominously, by several inches. Vincent and Citrine grabbed at the bars.

'Domne! It's the gulls,' said Vincent. 'When they take a fish, the barrel lightens, upsetting the balance.'

'If the fish are eaten, won't we just be lowered to the ground?' asked Citrine, her knuckles white from gripping the bars so tightly.

'No,' said Vincent. 'Look down.'

The growing morning light was casting a clearer picture of their predicament. What they had taken to be a solid floor

below them now showed itself to be a gaping hole that ran right through the centre of the lighthouse. At the bottom, a hundred feet down, there was only craggy rock.

'I see,' said Citrine slowly, trying to hide the terror creeping into her voice. 'The gulls take fish, the barrel side of the beam rises, our side lowers. Eventually the chain will just slide off completely and our cage will fall into the hole. We can't survive that.'

'Eventually? Surely just one fish will tip the balance. It could be the next one.'

'The straw that breaks the camel's back,' whispered Citrine.

'If I ever get my hands on Leucer or Leopold, they'll be sorry they tangled with me,' muttered Vincent. He looked all around him in futile desperation. For the first time in a long time, he could see no way out of the peril.

Another fish was taken.

The barrel end of the beam rose slightly.

The chain slid a few more inches, hastening their dreadful fate.

Vincent looked across at Citrine's pale face. She was saying something, but he could hardly hear it above the noise of the gulls.

'I've got an idea,' she shouted. 'But once we start there's no going back.'

Chapter 30
Countdown

On the shore of the Flumen, lit up intermittently by the lighthouse beam, Jonah and Folly were debating what to do. It was not easy to make themselves heard above the noise of the water and the wind and the screaming of the gulls.

'What's wrong with them?' asked Folly. 'They're making a Hades of a racket.'

They both looked at the lighthouse and the flock of birds circling the listing tower.

'That won't be standing much longer,' said Jonah. 'It's getting too dangerous to stay here.'

As if on cue, the lighthouse chose that moment to shudder and shift even further sideways. Jonah jumped to Folly's protection. She was staring at the tower, listening intently.

'Was that a human cry?'

'It can't be. No one's allowed up there. It must be the gulls,' said Jonah. 'We need to go to find the other two. They could be in danger. The sooner we get to Wincheap's the better.' He began to climb over the rocks, but Folly held back.

'I'm not sure they're going to be there.'

Jonah turned. 'What do you mean?'

'Your cards, they said you would be in danger in a high place. Well, the lighthouse is high. And something Axel said, about when he was being tortured by Kamptulicon and Leucer – "light coming and going". Maybe it was the lighthouse beam.'

Jonah frowned. 'What exactly are you saying?'

'I'm sure I heard a scream. Maybe this is where Leucer takes his prisoners. There could be someone up there. What if it's Citrine's father? Give me the glasses.'

Jonah handed them over and Folly trained them on the top of the lighthouse. As she watched, the towering edifice lurched again and part of the roof crashed into the Flumen with a tremendous splash, showering them with water.

'Flapping flatfish!' exclaimed Jonah, pulling at Folly's arm. 'We've got to go.'

But she shook him off. 'There *is* someone up there,' she said. 'At the window, I saw an arm. I'm sure of it.'

Jonah took the glasses and looked up to see the figures of Citrine and Vincent clambering on to the window's edge and standing hand in hand.'

'Domna,' breathed Folly. 'I think they're going to jump.'

*

Only moments earlier in the lighthouse the gulls had taken so many fish that, as Citrine had rightly predicted, the beam was at such an acute angle that the chain was fast approaching the end. But, by then, she and Vincent had set the cage in motion, swinging back and forth across the hole, so when the moment of truth finally came and the chain slid right off, instead of plunging the pair to certain death down the centre of the lighthouse, the cage flew off the end of the beam, overshot the hole and smashed against the lighthouse wall. The cage shattered and Vincent and Citrine lay stunned in the wreckage.

It took quite a few moments before the two of them were able to crawl from the twisted bars and take stock.

'We're alive,' whispered Citrine. 'I can't believe it.'

Vincent, who had dragged himself to a sitting position against the wall beside her, shook his head in disbelief. 'It worked – your idea worked,' he said.

Citrine opened her clenched palm and held it out to him. 'Maybe it was something to do with this.' She was holding his silver acorn.

More than a little overcome by emotion, Vincent and Citrine hugged and laughed for a few seconds, but they knew their ordeal was not yet over.

'Let's go,' said Vincent, helping Citrine to her feet. 'We might still be able to make our way out using the stairs.'

No sooner had he uttered the words than the lighthouse shifted again, even more violently than before, and they were thrown back against the wall. The tower was leaning like a severely listing ship; the curved wall had become the floor, and the floor had become a precipice. Outside, parts of the lighthouse masonry were breaking away and crashing into the water.

'Crawl around to the window,' said Vincent. 'Maybe we can jump.'

Together they made their painful way to the window, which was now at such an angle that it had effectively become a hole in the floor. In trepidation they looked out and their exhausted hearts sank. Through the flock of circling seagulls all they could see below them were the churning dark waters of the Flumen crashing on the jagged, black rocks.

'We can't jump,' said Citrine softly. 'It's certain death.'

The lighthouse groaned.

'We can't stay,' said Vincent simply.

'Then at least let's go together.'

They hauled themselves on to the window's edge and, hand in hand, stood there bloodied but unbowed.

'After three?' said Vincent.

Citrine started to count. 'One . . . two . . . th—'

Just as her tongue touched her lower lip to form the 'three',

something whizzed by her head so closely that it actually took out a hair.

'Domna,' she exclaimed. 'I've felt that before!'

And indeed she had! For the whizzing sound was made by Jonah's whale spear. The last time she had heard it fly past, Citrine's head was in the Carnifex's noose and she was on the verge of being hanged.

'Spletivus! It's Folly and Jonah,' cried Vincent, still teetering on the edge. 'They're down there on the shore.'

He looked behind him. The whale spear had shot through the window and embedded itself in the beam. It had a thick rope tied to its end with a sturdy whaler's knot.

'We can escape down the rope,' said Vincent urgently. 'Jonah's holding the other end. I'll hook my metal hand over it and we can slide down.'

'It's better than our other plan,' Citrine managed to joke as they tied themselves together using the cords that had earlier bound them. Vincent tested the rope, deemed it sufficiently taut (though he could hardly have deemed it otherwise under the circumstances), and together they launched themselves from the ledge into the unknown.

The metal hand, its fingers locked into a hook-like shape, slid rapidly down the length of the line with Vincent and Citrine dangling beneath. On the shore Jonah braced himself with every ounce of strength he possessed to keep the tension

on the rope. Folly held on to his belt and pulled from behind to give him extra purchase. The strain was beginning to tell.

'I don't think I can pull any harder,' gasped Folly, and she felt her feet starting to slip on the slimy rocks.

'Only a few more seconds,' panted Jonah. 'Hold tight.'

Then Vincent and Citrine suddenly loomed large before their rescuers and, just as their feet touched the shore, the lighthouse gave one last groan and toppled into the water.

CHAPTER 31
A QUEER QUARTET

In Leucer d'Avidus's study four men – the governor himself, Edgar Capodel, Professor Soanso and Leopold Kamptulicon – were busy congratulating themselves on a hugely successful and exciting evening.

'I thought the tremor in the middle only added to the atmosphere,' remarked Edgar.

'Indeed,' said the professor. 'I couldn't have asked for better timing! It gave the demonstration that little bit of extra tension. Kept the audience on the edge of their seats.'

'So, you think perhaps we three can work together?' enquired Leucer, topping up Arkwright's glass again. 'Kekrimpari and tar and chemicals seem such an ideal combination.'

'Oh yes, Governor,' replied the professor, slurring slightly.

Leucer put a friendly arm round his shoulder. 'Oh, call me Leucer, please! After all, we're going to get to know each other very well indeed. I can tell.'

'Now, Leucer, that old woman,' began Arkwright.

'A criminal and a fugitive, you say?'

'Oh, no need to worry about her. She is well and truly dealt with.'

'She seemed a little disturbed by proceedings.'

'Very disturbed,' chipped in Edgar. 'Belongs in the asylum. And another criminal was apprehended too, in the very act of robbing this house!'

Professor Soanso took a step back. 'Good lord! What a truly remarkable night!'

'Indeed,' said Kamptulicon. 'Two down, two to go. The Urban Guardsmen are waiting at the Kryptos. The others will be apprehended before sunrise.'

'Well, I propose a toast,' said Leucer. 'To what lies ahead.'

And all four touched glasses and each toasted his own vision of the future.

Chapter 32

Loose Ends and Secrets

The sounds of consternation and confusion were ringing around Mercator Square as the crowds mingled about the entrance to the Degringolade Playhouse and lingered in the streets. The show inside had been over for some time, but nobody wanted to go home. The startled audience didn't know quite what to make of the events they had witnessed. Ironically, the sight of the grey-haired woman running away seemed a fitting conclusion to Professor Soanso's attempt to revive a dead body. Some wondered if the old lady had not had a shot of kekrimpari herself. The atmosphere was further heightened by the rumour spreading that the lighthouse had fallen.

Away from the hubbub, in the back room of the Caveat Emptorium, Jonah, Folly, Citrine and Vincent were also in a state of disbelief, mainly on account of the fact that they were all still alive. Suma and Wenceslas were fussing over the foursome, pouring tea and attending to wounds and plying them with horsemeat-and-mustard sandwiches and hard cakes.

'So, Professor Soanso tried to revitalize a dead body with kekrimpari,' speculated Wenceslas. 'But how did they know you were there?'

'I think Edgar knew that there was a pretty good chance I would want to see the kekrimpari demonstration,' said Citrine quietly. 'If I had stayed quiet, I wouldn't have been found out, but I took their bait. How could I not say something? The thought of my poor father being subjected to such . . . such wickedness.'

'Despicable,' said Suma. 'Edgar rooted you out by appealing to your devotion to your father. He is beyond contempt.'

'That's if it even was Hubert,' said Jonah.

'I really couldn't see, but I was so shocked at the time, and after all that has happened, that I actually believed Edgar might be telling the truth.'

'What about Leucer? You say he sneaked out. How could he have known that Vincent was planning to go to the Governor's Residence?'

'Well, I saw this in the *Degringolade Daily* the other day,' said Suma quietly. 'I wonder if that might have something to do with it.' She held up the paper, folded to show the article about the governor's new safe.

'I didn't see that,' said Folly with a frown.

Vincent pulled the same article from his pocket. 'I tore it

out,' he said. 'I wanted to leave it in the safe when I took the Blivet. A message to Leucer.'

Folly looked at him in astonishment and tutted loudly. 'More like a message to you! You do realize it was a trap?'

Vincent threw up his hands. 'OK, so I flamped, I messed it all up, I failed,' he began, but Folly cut him off.

'It's all right. I know you can't help it. It's like an addiction. You just can't resist a challenge.'

Vincent reddened ever so slightly and began to pat his hair, ostensibly to remove the dust and dirt from the lighthouse collapse, but really to conceal his embarrassment. Folly was right, but he wasn't going to admit it. Then something flew out of his hair and landed at Suma's feet. She picked it up.

'It's a silver cufflink,' she said. 'And it's engraved – "HNC".'

Citrine sat bolt upright. 'HNC? Hubert Nathaniel Capodel! It's my father's. Vincent, where in Aether did you get this?'

He shook his head. 'I don't know. At the lighthouse maybe, when it started to crumble. There was stuff flying about all over the place.'

'What was my father doing in the lighthouse?' wondered Citrine as she placed the cufflink in her locket. 'Well, I made

a promise to myself not to give up on finding out what happened to him. Until I have real proof that he is dead, I will continue to believe that he is alive.'

'Speaking of lighthouses,' said Suma, addressing Jonah and Folly, 'what I really want to know is how you two found your way to the lighthouse.'

'The Puca told me the way.'

Suma's eyes widened and Wenceslas's mouth gaped. 'The Puca told you?'

Folly nodded and adopted her inscrutable expression, the one that defied anyone to probe any further.

Suma said no more, but looked as if there was plenty she could say, and Wenceslas slapped his thigh heartily. 'Well, it seems to me you've all had more than your fair share of Degringolade luck.'

'Thanks to you, Wenceslas, in no small part,' said Jonah humbly. 'Those glasses you gave me saved all our lives. I even managed to get my whale spear back from the river.'

Citrine sighed. 'I still have to prove my innocence.'

'I might not have got the Blivet this time,' said Vincent rather defiantly, 'but at least we know now for sure that Leucer has it.'

'And what about you, Folly?' asked Suma in that knowing way of hers. 'Have you made any promises to anyone or anything?'

Vincent looked directly at the leather-clad, Blivet-wielding Supermundane hunter (in many ways all that he himself wanted to be), but Folly just shrugged and didn't answer. He chewed on his lip thoughtfully. There was at least *one* promise he could think of: the one she had made to Axel. As for the Puca, he just knew there was more to that encounter than she was telling.

In his pocket his hand slipped again through the hole in the lining and his fingers closed round the silver compact. Instantly he remembered the dream. He heard Lady Degringolade's voice again, as if she was right beside him, and it sent a cold thrill down his spine.

'*You will know when to come.*'

Folly, for once, averted her gaze from Vincent's penetrating stare. Suma's question was unnervingly close to the bone. What exactly did the wily old woman know about dealing with the Puca? Had she guessed the bargain that had been struck? Folly could barely bring herself to think on it. But she had had no choice. She could not have escaped the tunnels, or saved Jonah, without the Puca's help. As for the deal, how could she have known that it would happen so quickly, that *she* would rise from the dead? Folly had so hoped that she had imagined the woman in the tunnel, but when she looked down at her boot and saw the stain, the stain that wouldn't rub away, the stain of the beast's saliva,

she knew that it had all been very real.

Now she must honour her promise . . . and bring to the Puca the head of Lady Scarletta Degringolade.

Or face certain death.

Chapter 33
The Mistress of the Manor

Far away from the Caveat Emptorium, where the Phenomenals were mulling over their respective problems and secrets, and far too from the Governor's Residence, where success was being celebrated, another performer in the complicated drama playing out in Degringolade was pondering her own fate.

Lady Scarletta Degringolade, with faithful Katatherion at her side, was standing at the top of the once magnificent staircase of Degringolade Manor. And her haughty gaze fell not on the all-encompassing decrepitude of her former home but on the quivering horde of Pluriba below awaiting her instruction.

'Home, sweet, home,' she murmured. 'It's been too long.'

GLOSSARY

Adderstone – a type of stone, usually glassy

Aether – heaven

Ambergris – aka 'floating gold', stone-like lumps of whale vomit, used to control Lurids and other Superents

Antikamnial – liquid painkiller

Apogee – the lunar apogee is when the moon is at the furthest point in its orbit from the earth (see perigee)

Autandron – a sort of robot

Black beans – used to distract Superents, they are compelled to pick them up

Blivet – a specialized weapon for repelling Superents, platinum with three prongs; *verb* to bliv

Brinepurse – a purse for carrying salt crystals to repel Lurids and other Superents

Browpin – like an earring but worn through the brow by Degringoladians for luck

Cachelot – (pron. *ca-sha-low* or *catch-a-lot*) a rare species of whale

Caligo – the name for the thirteenth month in the Degringoladian calendar

Card-spreading – the practice of 'reading' illustrated cards to aid decision-making and to predict the future

Carnifex – the hangman

Caveat Emptorium – a type of swap shop, akin to a pawnshop, from the Latin expression '*caveat emptor*' ('let the buyer beware')

Claptrapulation – 'nonsense' (thought to be Irish in origin, peculiar to Julianstown, Meath)

Corvid – large black bird, similar to crow or rook

Crex – 'evening'; one of the four segments in the Degringoladian day, the others being Lux (morning), Prax (afternoon), Nox (night)

Cunningman – a master of the Supermundane and practitioner of the Furtivartes

Domna – an interjection used by Degringoladian women

Domne – an interjection used by Degringoladian men

DUG – (abbr.) Degringolade Urban Guard, the Degringolade security force, members referred to as 'Urgs' (derogatory)

Ergastirion – a Cunningman's workshop

Festival of Lurids – an annual festival intended to appease the Lurids on the Tar Pit

Firestrike – similar to a match, often referred to by brand, 'Fulger's'

Flamp – (verb) means to try but fail at an impossible task

(attributed to Erin Tosh from Aberdeen, winner of The Phenomenals Invent-a-Word competition)

Flumen – the river that runs around Degringolade and flows into the Turbid Sea

Furtivartes – Rituals and ceremonies associated with the Supermundane

Gevra – the coldest of the four seasons in Antithica Province, followed by Torock, Savra, Faur (equivalent to winter, spring, summer, autumn)

Ghouze – a liquefied Supermundane substance consisting of particles called Minuscules; Superents are composed of ghouze

Grainwine – a strong, clear alcoholic drink

Hades – 'Hell' e.g. 'What the Hades is going on?'

Impedimentium – a magnetic ore, in plentiful supply under the salt marsh and Tar Pit in Degringolade

Katatherion – a Supermundane beast that slumbers underground until required by its master or mistress

Kekrimpari – an energy source discovered by Professor Arkwright Soanso

Kew – 'thank you' (colloquial)

Kite Wagon – a type of gypsy caravan characterized by its sloping walls, wider at the top than the bottom

Klepteffigium – (Greek and Latin) a device similar to a basic camera; literally 'image stealer'

Komaterion – cemetery

Kronometer – landmark clock tower in Degringolade, situated in Mercator Square

Kryptos – (*pl.* Kryptoi) burial chamber

Leech barometer – a weather-predicting device containing leeches whose movements can be interpreted to predict the weather

Lux – See *Crex*

Maerl – ossified seaweed used to make the specialized multifaceted dice used in card-spreading

Mangledore – the pickled left hand of a criminal, usually a murderer, thought to have Supermundane properties

Manufactory – factory

Manuslantern – hand-held oil lamp

Memento mori – (Latin) literally 'remember that you will die'; a symbolic or artistic reminder of mortality

Nany/nanyone/nanything – (colloquial) not any, no one, nothing

Narkos – a sleep-inducing potion

Natron – specialized salt to repel Superents, more effective than normal salt

Nox – see *Crex*

Omnia Intum – literally 'all things within'; a Cunningman's handbook of rituals, recipes and aspects of the Furtivartes

Pedalate – technical term used in relation to a Trikuklos, using the pedals to move the vehicle

Perigee (see *Apogee*) – the point in the moon's orbit when it is nearest the earth

Prax – see *Crex*

Propinquity – (Latin) the state of being close to something or someone, similar to 'proximity'

Puca – elusive, mischievous spirits, seen as blue flames, inhabiting the salt marsh (aka 'Palus Salus') to the west of Degringolade. They lead unwitting travellers off the path into danger

Quodlatin – a form of Latin used in Omnia Intums (*also* Inta), similar to Latin but deliberately misleading and open to interpretation

Sal volatile – a chemical compound used to arouse consciousness

Sella Subjunctum – literally 'Chair of Subjection', aka torture chair; used to 'persuade' the occupant to confess or give up information and in Supermundane ceremonies

Sequart – see *sequentury*

Sequentury – coin in the monetary system of Antichica Province. Sequenturies are divided into four sequarts and ten sequins

Sequin – see *sequentury*

Slumgullion – a type of stew

Smitelight – a hand-held light, activated and deactivated by tapping

Spergo – (Quodlatin) a liquid that causes temporary blindness

Spletivus – an interjection

Stunner – walnut-sized explosive, creates bright light and stuns enemy

Sylvan Beluae – bear-like creatures that inhabit woods

Superents – (abbr.) Supermundane Entities, the name given to mainly malignant creatures that exist in the world of the Supermundane

Phenomenals – particularly malevolent Superents, usually found in groups

Lurids – restless shades of executed convicts

Noctivagrantes – (sing. Noctivagrant) vicious invisible Superents who hunt in packs, often underground

Pluribus – (*pl.* Pluriba) globular greenish Superents, usually solitary, exist above ground

Hypnagogue – generally benign Superent that leads a person into sleep

Hypnopomp – generally benign Superent that leads a person out of sleep

Supermundane – broadly similar to the concept of 'the Supernatural', a parallel world outside normalcy, causing inexplicable events; the origin of Superents

Tar Pit – a treacherous lake of tar in the salt marsh surrounded by toxic gases generally necessitating the use of gas masks

Temptatious – tempting

Treen – a term used for items made from wood

Trikuklos – (*pl.* Trikukloi) a sophisticated three-wheeled vehicle

Troika – a luxurious vehicle pulled by three horses abreast

Turbid Sea – the sea into which the river Flumen flows, that washes the shores of Degringolade

Vanitas painting – a still-life painting characterized by objects representing man's mortality, e.g. a skull and items in a state of decline

Vulgar – term used to describe people not initiated into the Supermundane

Look out for another dark and twisted adventure in

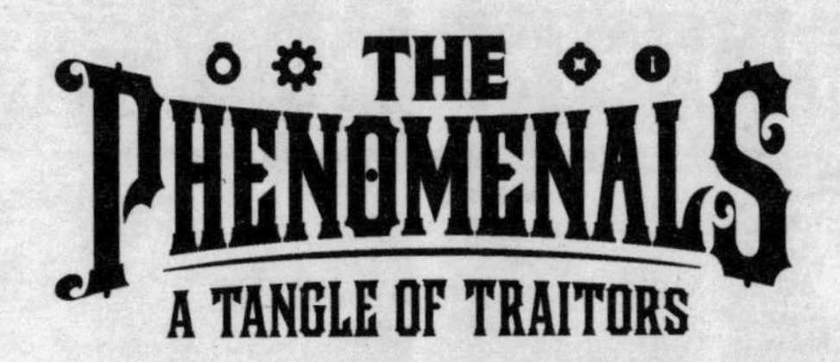

F.E. HIGGINS

Read more **BLOODTHIRSTY**, **SHOCKING** and **GRUSEOME** stories in . . .

TALES FROM THE SINISTER CITY

F.E. HIGGINS